Pope Joan

EMMANUEL ROÏDES

Pope Joan

Translated by
David Connolly

AIORA

Co-funded by the
Creative Europe Programme
of the European Union

Published with the support of the Kostas and Helen Ouranis Foundation.

David Connolly is retired Professor of Translation Studies at the Aristotle University of Thessaloniki. He has translated over fifty books with works by contemporary Greek writers. His translations have received awards in the USA, the UK and Greece.

Original title: *Ἡ Πάπισσα Ἰωάννα*

© Aiora Press 2019

ISBN: 978-618-5369-18-7

First edition October 2019

AIORA PRESS
11 Mavromichali St.
Athens 10679, Greece
www.aiorabooks.com

TRANSLATOR'S PREFACE

Emmanuel Roïdes (Roidis, Rhoides, Royidis) was born in 1836 on the Greek island of Syros into a wealthy family originally from Chios. He was still young when his family moved to Genoa, where his father had been assigned to the Greek Consulate and where he lived through the revolutions of 1848 and the revolt of Genoa. He returned to Syros in 1849 and completed his schooling there, before leaving once again to pursue his university studies in history, literature and philosophy first in Germany and later in Romania. He subsequently returned to Greece to live in Athens where, apart from a brief stay in Egypt, he spent the rest of his life until his death in 1904. His family wealth enabled him to enjoy a carefree, aristocratic life until the family business foundered in the stock-market crisis of 1880. Reduced to near-poverty in his later life, he was obliged to find work and earned a meagre living as a librarian in the National Library of Greece. He is best known for his novel, *Pope Joan*, but most of his literary work was as an essayist, critic and translator.[1] He also wrote a number of short stories, many of which were set in his native island of Syros.[2] He is regarded today as one of the classic authors of modern Greek literature.

Pope Joan, or *Papissa Ioanna* as is the title of the book in Greek, was presented by Roïdes as a "medieval study". It is based on the story that first appeared in 13th-century chronicles and later spread throughout Europe of a female pope, who reigned, according to some sources, from 855 to 857 AD. Different versions of the story describe her as a talented and learned woman who disguised herself as a man in order to enter the Church and follow her lover. Because of her exceptional abilities, she soon rose through the church hierarchy and was eventually elected pope. Her sex was discovered when she gave birth during a religious procession and she is said to have died shortly after. The story was widely believed for centuries, but today it is generally regarded as fictional.[3] In his preface "To the Reader",

---

[1] Notably of Chateaubriand's *Itinéraires* (1860) and Lord Macaulay's five-volume *History of England* (1897-1902). He was also the first translator into Greek of works by Edgar Allen Poe.

[2] A selection of these have been translated into English by Petros Kronis and published as *Emmanuel's Travels* (2012).

[3] The legend of the female pope has, indeed, been a popular subject for fictional works. Prior to Roïdes' novel is the play by Ludwig Achim von Arnim, *Päpstin Johanna* (1813) and the novel by Wilhelm Smets, *Das Mährchen von der Päpstin Johanna auf's Neue erörtert* (1829). More recent novels include: Marjorie Bowen's *Black Magic* (1909), Ludwig Gorm's *Päpstin Johanna* (1912), Marietta Giannopoulou-Minotou's fictional biography (1931), Donna Woolfolk Cross' *Pope Joan* (1996), Yves Bichet's *La Papesse Jeanne* (2005) and Hugo N. Gerstl's *Scribe: The Story of the Only Female Pope* (2005). Worth noting,

Roïdes describes how he heard the story from the mouth of a newspaper editor while in a cellar in Genoa, sheltering from the siege guns of Victor Emmanuel, and how, fascinated by the story, he later researched the historical facts surrounding it in the library of Berlin.

Published in 1866 (with successive editions in 1879 and 1882), Roïdes' *Pope Joan* immediately caused a sensation because of its caustic criticism of the Catholic clergy of the time and of the Church's traditions and customs, for the book is not just a portrait of Joan, but paints a tapestry of her entire age. Surprisingly, it was the Greek Orthodox Church that took offence, perceiving its own clergy as being the real target of this criticism and its own traditions and customs as being the object of ridicule and satire in the loosely-veiled comparison Roïdes makes between the medieval times he describes and his own times. Consequently, the Holy Synod denounced the book and anathematized it. Roïdes himself seems to have been quite indifferent to this, although, in later editions of the work, he takes pains to point out to his critics that all the facts and events related in the book are based on indisputable testimonies and that his descriptions of life in the monasteries, of church rituals and theological doctrines are all taken from medieval sources and are the result of extensive historical research.

As might be expected, the controversy surrounding the book only enhanced Roïdes' fame, while the book

---

too, are the two films based on the legend of Pope Joan directed by Michael Anderson (1972) and Sönke Wortman (2009), the latter based on Cross' novel.

itself was soon translated into other European languages. It enjoyed a huge success, for example, in France, where the translation of 1878 went through seven reprints in only three years and was notably re-translated by Alfred Jarry and Jean Saltas in 1908. In England, two translations of the work appeared during Roïdes' lifetime: the one by Charles Hastings Collette (1886) and the other by J. H. Freese (1900). It was presumably in one of these translations that the work was known and admired by Mark Twain. The work was re-translated in the 20th century by T.D. Kriton (1935) and achieved further notoriety in the English-speaking world in the rather free and racy translation by Lawrence Durrell (1954).

In Greece, the book remained for a long time the subject of scathing criticism or, at best, a cause for perplexity among critics, who were at pains to classify it in terms of genre (historical study, romance, parody, satire?). Apart from the criticism relating to its irreverence, anticlericalism and bawdiness, it was criticized for its borrowings, its often outlandish similes and a style that was far removed from the romantic norms of the day, at which Roïdes constantly pokes fun. In more recent times, however, it has come to be admired for its elegant and rhetorical style, for its inventive and striking similes and for its irony and wittiness. Roïdes' distorted and often incorrect references to Biblical passages, for which he was criticized in the past, are now more properly seen as a deliberate part of his overall satirical and subversive intentions and, in this, the work is notably modernist in its outlook and anti-conformism. Even his playful asides to the reader are very modern in their subversive and tongue-in-cheek effect. Today, the book is generally regarded as a comic masterpiece of modern Greek literature and remains ever relevant for its satire on both secular and religious authority.

This brief translator's preface would be incomplete without a mention of Roïdes' choice of linguistic idiom and its consequences for the translator. When the Greek State was established following the 1821 War of Independence, one of the burning questions concerned what the language of the new State should be. Opinions were divided between supporters of the existing spoken language (demotic) and supporters of a return to ancient attic Greek. Katharevousa, an artificial language purified of foreign (mainly Turkish) words, represented something of a compromise between these two tendencies and was eventually adopted as the standard form of written Greek and remained the official language of the Greek State until 1976, though demotic remained as the everyday spoken language. It was katharevousa that Roïdes consciously chose to use for his literary works. In the prologue to his translation of Chateaubriand, he explains that having been brought up and educated abroad and consequently unversed in the (demotic) language of the people, he preferred to use katharevousa while, at the same time, expressing his reservations about this artificial language.[4]

His use of katharevousa cannot be adequately reproduced in English, which contains no corresponding phases in its historical evolution and no corresponding

---

[4] Similarly, in a letter to Panagiotis Vergiotis, he writes: "I make use of the so-called katharevousa not by choice, but of necessity, given that I was late in coming to Greece from abroad and I learned the language from books as a dead language, not being versed in the popular language of the people…"

linguistic idiom.[5] Given that it was the standard literary
idiom of his day, it might be argued (as some people do)
that it might simply be translated into standard literary
English, whether of the present day or of the mid-19th
century. Nevertheless, to many contemporary Greek
readers it is a language no longer easily comprehensible,
as is evidenced by the translations of the works by Roïdes[6]
and by other 19th-century Greek authors, such as Papa-
diamantis and Vizyenos, into the contemporary Greek
language. My approach has been to adopt a somewhat
"stylized" English idiom including archaisms in an attempt to give a taste, at least, of what contemporary
Greek readers experience in their reading of Roïdes.

The text translated here is that contained in: Emmanuel Roïdes, *Papissa Ioanna*. The first complete fac-
simile of the original edition of 1866 with a biographical
and critical foreword by Tassos Vournas (Athens: Tolides
1971). Also included is the translation of Roïdes' preface
"To the Reader", but not his "Introduction", which has
been omitted in keeping with his own suggestion for
those not particularly "enamoured of historical discussions, somnolence and references", but also in order not

---

[5] Contemporary Greek authors are able to use an admixture of
demotic and katharevousa, which sometimes results in a learned
tone, sometimes irony, sometimes humour, sometimes bombast.
In such cases, the translator into English can at least attempt to
reproduce these effects using appropriate linguistic means.

[6] By Dimitris Kalokyris (Athens: Ellinika Grammata 2005). It
should be noted that this and other translations of 19th-century
authors were not without their share of controversy, with strong
views expressed on both sides as to the necessity for translations
of works written less than 150 years earlier.

to overburden the present volume. For the same reasons, the copious endnotes to the text provided by Roïdes have also been omitted. All the footnotes to references in the text are by the author unless otherwise stated.

Durrell, in the preface to his translation of the book, quotes George Katsimbalis (Henry Miller's "Colossus of Maroussi") as saying about Roïdes' *Papissa Ioanna*: "Now there's a good book… It is a typical scamp of a book, a Greek book, full of good fun, bad taste, and laughter and irreverence." Let the "dear reader" decide whether it remains so in this new translation.

David Connolly
Athens 2019

Pope Joan

To the Reader

At the beginning of his *Histories*, Herodotus considered it prudent to outline the reasons that motivated him to relate the triumphs of Miltiades and the "caprine" loves of the Egyptian women. Later historians, Thucydides, Tacitus, St. Luke, Gibbon and Guizot, hastened to imitate the good example of the father of history; consequently, all histories invariably begin with the historian's justification, just as epics do with an appeal to the Muse. Bowing to this historic rule and so as not to be accused of being a fanciful grave-robber, I, too, hasten to explain how I came to disturb the slumber of Pope Joan, resting in peace as she has been now for so many centuries.

Religious feeling in the West was still at its height (that is, there were still people who ate lobster on Fridays and kissed the hem of the priest's cassock) when, some twenty years ago, still in the bloom of youth, I travelled to Italy. Living for many months of the year in the countryside in keeping with the local custom out of love of the rural life, often during the long autumnal evenings while the snails were crawling upon the bare vines and the mushrooms were sprouting beneath the chestnut trees and while I was sitting beside the fire of the harvesters, from whom I heard nothing but of the miracles of holy icons, the escape of vampires from their tombs and of souls from purgatory, I had, because of this association with rural folk, grown quite credulous; and I thought that the Pope, who, so I heard, opened and closed the gates of Paradise, who enjoyed the most cordial of relationships with the Holy Spirit which came down upon his shoulder every morning, and who proffered his holy feet for the temporal kings to kiss, was an enormous and mythical being hovering like a hot-air balloon between heaven and earth.

It was in just such a mental state that I found myself, while living in Genoa, when in 1848 the revolution broke out that would send shockwaves through the whole of Italy. Religion and the clergy were included, as is the case in all political upheavals in the West, in the imprecations against kings and tyranny. An evil wind had been blowing for a number of years over this unfortunate peninsula, filling all hearts with displeasure, disobedience and an unquenchable thirst for freedom. Thrones teetered ready to fall; their royal occupants even more so. Inconsonant words, alien to Italian ears, such as "constitution", "militia", "free press"

and "joint ownership" echoed from all sides like the
hissing of vipers. And as for blind faith, accustomed for
countless centuries to the compassion and attention of
the blind, this was ousted as a troublesome beggar and,
terrified, made for the mountains, seeking refuge beneath the roofs of peasants and indeed often finding
their doors shut and barred. Yet while this poor wretch
was wandering in the dark, stumbling with every step,
the kings whose power this wretch supported did not
remain idle; the rebelling Genoa was put under siege,
the shells blasted the roofs of the houses, while the
poor inhabitants, terrified lest they suffer the same fate
as the roofs, sought refuge where, below ground, were
kept the most fragile of all utensils; the bottles. It was to
such a wine cellar that I, too, betook myself in the middle of the night together with my family and neighbours, who had come to seek refuge under the folds
of the Greek flag.[1] More than fifty, men and women,
gentry and fishmongers, countesses and coalmen, all
squeezed together in that narrow place, between bottles and crocks, onions and dried figs. The shells of
Victor Emmanuel, failing in their tyrannical purpose
to kill the populace, destroyed nevertheless the old bas-
tions of social inequality, bringing together his pallid
subjects in a democratic fraternity of fear. Initially, the
gloom and silence of the graveyard prevailed in that

---

[1] Trans. note: the cellar was in the Greek Consulate, where the
author's father worked.

subterranean assembly. But the house consisted of five
storeys and the vaults of the wine-cellar were sound
and inaccessible to the shells so that the faces around
me, hitherto pale-green like the glass of the surrounding bottles, gradually assumed a more human colour.
And so, almost fearlessly, we listened to the terrible
sounds on the ground above, confident that, however
much it stooped, death would be unable to reach us
down below. With the removal of the danger, the tied
tongues of the Italians gradually became loosened; the
echo in the vault repeated incoherent words, promises
of candles lit to the Madonna, arguments between the
men, appeals to saints and terrible curses against
the *Bombardatore*. Yet just as in the battles of Ariosto,
when two renowned heroes engage in combat, and the
rest of the warriors lower their arms watching the
combat in silence, so also, one after the other, those in
the wine cellar fell silent when the grizzled Abbot of
St. Matthew's and the aged editor of the *Genoa News*,
sitting opposite each other on facing barrels, began
quarrelling about liberty and kingship, about progress
and papism. The events taking place up above us rendered this discussion most timely, while the adversaries were both well versed in such combats and the
audience encircled them with mouths and ears open
just as the Carthaginians with Aeneas. The journalist
maintained that all the sufferings to which we were
being subjected were as a result of the influence of the
clergy, while the abbot insisted on seeing the fraternal
blood flowing all around us as a propitiatory sacrifice

to the Supreme Being. The night, however, was progressing and the discussion did not appear to be drawing any nearer to a close. The tongues swished sharply and scathingly like gladiators' swords. Gradually becoming accustomed to all this verbal din, I soon succumbed to an involuntary stupor, resting my head of just ten years on the lap of the woman next to me, when suddenly a strange noise drove the sleep from my eyelids. The irascible newspaperman, finally losing his patience at the abbot's obstinacy, who responded to the most cogent of arguments with church maxims and passages from Bonaldo and Demaitre, changed his tactics. Desperate to open the eyes of that blessed man, who feared the light as much as bats do the rays of the sun, he ceased his reasoned discussion and was already attempting to present the other's position to those listening as being detestable and ridiculous. Opening the dirtiest pages of papal history and gathering together every kind of ignominy and stain contained therein, he spat it out like a viper into the face of the poor priest. He presented to us Benedict IX, Gregory VI and Sylvester III, contemporaneous popes, as a three-headed Cerberus, each excommunicating the other and plunging Italy into a sea of blood; Zacharias as condemning to the flames those geographers who taught the existence of the antipodes, for in the abundance of his knowledge, for there to be antipodes, there would have to exist two suns and a double moon; Stephen VII as a despicable grave-robber for exhuming the body of his predecessor Formosus, dragging the rotted corpse before the synod and subjecting it to an abominable and ridiculous interrogation; John XXII as wasting his life in pursuit of the philosopher's stone and finally discovering this through the drawing up of a list which noted the exact price for forgiving every type of sin, murder, rape or other; Julius III as a latter-day Caligula, ordaining his monkey, amidst wine-cups and women, as a cardinal; and John XII as placing the Holy Altar cloths at the feet of his mistress, getting drunk with her using the holy chalices and, finally, being murdered by his wife, who discovered them, or by the devil, as the chroniclers would have it, though certainly there is some common characteristic between the devil and a wife played false. This, then, is what the old man said amid the deep silence, occasionally interrupted by the explosion of a shell nearby or the collapse of some roof. A goodly number of those listening were making the holy sign of the cross, others covered their ears and the women hid their faces in their aprons; but what shall I say of myelf when the unrelenting orator, no longer satisfied with just the outrageous behaviour of the male popes, began to relate the tale of Pope Joan? Of the love and maternity of a pope and her childbirth in the midst of the marketplace!

Presently, the day dawned; the explosions lessened and gradually ceased. Invincible Genoa capitulated following three days of siege and surrendered the leaders of the revolution, which the very next day was renamed sedition, into the clutches of the tyrant, as they

then called Victor. The peddlers disguised as militia-
men, the tenors and bases of the melodrama, who had
removed the make-up from their cheeks and had
girdled on their medieval swords chanting "Freedom
or Death" in the streets together with the students
priding themselves that alone with their law books and
medical books as weapons they were capable of fend-
ing off the tyrant's swords all vanished at the first flash
of the royal lances like the crows of night as soon as
the sun rises. And as for the Italian women who had
sewn flags and woven tricoloured ribbons, they once
again remembered the counsels of their confessors,
and if any officer were to kiss them in the marketplace,
they turned the other cheek in vilification. After only a
few days, red flags and freedom hymns and martyrs'
blood and bullets and ruins were all forgotten. Yet
it was impossible for me to forget the popess. The odd
circumstances in which I had learned of her, the
strange manner of the speaker, the cellar, the fear, the
massacre up above, all this rendered the impression
left on my heart as indelible as the footsteps of the
Saviour on the stony ground of Judaea.

Since then, Joan's doleful shade has often visited
me in sleep, holding a stillborn babe in her arms; while
in the daytime I sought in every way to learn more
concerning this singular heroine. First I asked the
teachers, the servants, the peasant digging the ditches,
the Capuchins begging for much more than a mite,
spending long hours in the libraries breathing the dust
of worm-eaten tomes in the hope of finding some

trace, which with such diligence the Italian clergy had erased, of my popess so that after great toil, after having screeched like Caesar's parrot *Tempus et labor oleunt* and not having found a crumb of evidence, my curiosity finally died of hunger.

A few years later, I found myself in Berlin, still unversed in the use of pipe-smoking, beer and public places and consequently at a loose end and isolated among all the extremely busy foreign students. Boredom and idleness are, as I have often since observed, the main, if not the sole, causes of love, capable in the absence of new passions of rekindling old ones. Some such thing happened with my memory of Pope Joan. One festive morning, when the Berlin sky, wishing it seems to affirm the text of Moses, sent forth a deluge, I took refuge in the deserted library and, dragging my tedium and ennui from one room to the next, I suddenly found myself in a huge arcade in which were theological books from the middle ages, all wrapped in a thick layer of white dust, like shrouded corpses in their deep and peaceful sleep. The smell of cheese reminds the Swiss of their homeland, that of straw the asses their stable, and that of flowers the lovers their beloved; as for me the smell of the old paper awakened the memory of the popess. "Here," I said, gazing at those dust-covered stacks, "lies the solution to the riddle that has so preoccupied me." And obtaining permission and a cloth from the curator to open and dust those mildewed voluminous books, I began tome by tome and page by page to search for traces of my heroine. And with the help of the collection of *Rerum Germanicarum*, of the catalogues of Dufresne and of the dissertations by Bayle and von Spanheim, I was able in the space of a few months

> *Veterum volvens monumentia virorum*

to get through and collect in two large exercise books most of what, over the past eight centuries, has been written in support or in vilification of the female pope. But at that time such was my inexperience in these matters of research that I was often obliged to peruse an entire chapter or every page of a tome before my eyes came to rest on the passage I was seeking, thus unintentionally learning of numerous odd details concerning religion, habits and customs during those dark centuries.

This is the genesis of Pope Joan, which for five years I had left to the presses of my imagination, and then,

> *Venutomi inanzi*
> *Un che di stampar libri lavora*
> *Dissi stampami questo alla malora.*[2]

On beginning to write, I immediately perceived how dry and tedious a simple historical account of everything relating to Joan would be for most people, given that the majority of readers were ignorant even of her

---

[2] Berni.

existence. So confining this part of the work to the Introduction,[3] I transformed the rest of the book into a kind of narrative encyclopaedia of the middle ages and of the ninth century in particular.

By virtue of the poets, writers and artists, every age from the very creation of our planet and every country it contains is more or less known to all. Every age and every people has left us monuments depicting the people of the time; the Hebrews the Sacred Scripture, the Egyptians the pyramids and the Greeks the *Iliad*. From Eve, whose loves were sung by Moses and Milton, to Cymodocée, whose martyr's garland was woven by Chateaubriand, the chain is virtually unbroken. In which age can the wayfarer find refuge and on which shore can he find repose without encountering familiar smiling faces, friends holding out a hand to him? Rachel offering water to his parched lips or Nausicaa leading him to some hospitable abode? But dismounting from our Pegasus before he becomes unshod, we should note that everyone knows the beards of the Patriarchs, the robes of the Greek philosophers, the phalanxes of the Macedonians, the blond wigs of the concubines of Rome, the tattooed skin of the northern barbarians, the rosaries of the Christian martyrs and everything else described by the poets and writers as these were taught in school or read in translation. Even

---

[3] Trans. note: not included in the present volume as explained in the translator's preface.

more familiar are the ironclad heroes emerging at the end of the middle ages and the white-garbed heroines, the Amadeus', the Tristans, the Lionhearted, the Templars, the Abenserages, the Iolandas the Herminas and the Armides, whose symbols, armour, loves and feats are known to all from the works of Walter Scott, the verses of Victor Hugo, the collections in the museums and the songs of Rossini and Mayerbeer. Yet from the sixth to the eleventh century, from the last Roman emperor to the first knight, who were the people inhabiting our planet? What did they do, what did they eat, what did they believe and what did they wear? This question can only be answered by the professional historian, one undertaking the thankless task of perusing through the huge collections of the medieval chroniclers, the mildewed *Legendaries*, the largely indigestible drivel of the monks, the writings of Cassiodorus, Caesarius, Alcuin, St. Agobard, Rabanus Maurus and innumerable other books known only to the learned and the worms, to which Mouratori refers as *Sterili steppe della leteratura del medio evo*, or sterile wastelands of medieval literature. It was in these wastelands that I found myself wandering in search of some trace of Joan. And just as the traveller who visits distant and undiscovered parts likes to take from each some memento of his wanderings, a leaf from the tree casting its shadow over a desert well, a shell from some shore unbeknown to sailors or a flower blossoming on some untrodden peak, so I, too, from each of these volumes condemned to eternal oblivion took as a memento some passage describing forgotten customs, strange ideas, folk superstitions, remnants of idolatry and whatever else had escaped the notice of later historians, who, engaged as they are with general theories, have no other aim than to historically justify the tenets of the group to which they belong and for whom such details are of no use or interest. Using the stones I gathered from these obscure sources, I put together or attempted to put together a mosaic that would present an image as realistic as possible of that dark era, concerning which, as far as I know, no book accessible to all has ever been diligently written, rendering it known and translucent like *The Fortunes of Telemachus* did for heroic Greece, *The Testimonies* for the decline of Rome and *Ivanhoe* for chivalric England. Immediately realising that my powers were insufficient for such a task and how inferior I was to those who had undertaken something of the sort, I decided that I would take pride at least in not being inferior in terms of historical accuracy. Thus, every sentence in *Pope Joan*, virtually every word, is based on the testimony of some modern author. The monastic anecdotes are taken from the chronicles of the contemporary monasteries, the miracles from the medieval *Legendaries*, the description of the rituals from the letters of Einhard, Alcuin and the ecclesiastical History of Gregory of Tours, the strange theological doctrines from the writings of the contemporary theologians St. Agobard, Hincmar, Rabanus and others; every description of towns, buildings, clothing or food is precise in the minutest detail, as can be seen in part from the endnotes to the work,[4] which might easily have been many more, but before one renders his book more voluminous, he first has to know whether or not it will be read. And I refer here to this not to show the breadth of my learning, but rather to show how much I respect my readers. And this respect for the reader, so foreign and unprecedented in our country, is worthy, in my opinion, of the favorable reception reserved for foreigners by all civilized people.

Yet this respect for the reader, albeit a worthy virtue, like some *pater familias* clad in the garb of a militiaman, is not sufficient, for, apart from this, the readers also demand of the author that he should not send them to sleep. Printed pages have the same effect on the Greek reader as the leaves of the hyoscyamus; and perhaps for this reason most people are afraid even to touch them, but rather bequeath our literary products pure and unsullied to the next generations. It was Swift, the English author, I think, who recounts how the inhabitants of some place I don't recall are so indifferent and inattentive that whenever someone addresses them, he has to hit them on the head every so often with a dry pumpkin so that they don't fall asleep while he is talking. I, too, thought to employ just such a sleep-repellant against the indifference of the Greek reader; and for lack of a pumpkin, to attempt

---

[4] Trans. note: the author's copious endnotes have been omitted in this volume as explained in the translator's preface.

to stifle their yawns by having recourse on every page to sudden digressions, odd similes or unusual word combinations; encasing every idea in an almost tangible image, adorning even the most serious theological matters with crochet, tassels and bells like the costume of a Spanish dancer. This mode of writing, introduced to the English by Byron, to the Germans by Heine and to the French by Murger and Musset, was invented by the Italian decadent poets, who, desperate to scale the peaks on which Dante and Petrarch had affixed their flags, sought a different path, leading not to glory but to popularity. This literature resembles in truth the flirting of those women, who, lacking in beauty or numbering more years than teeth, seek in diverse ways, through cosmetics, smiles, false promises and open cleavages to attract, in the absence of pure love, the desire or at least the curiosity of the onlookers. I have no intention here either of praising this school or recommending it; but only through the use of such salt did I believe it was possible to season that most unpalatable of all foods: medieval ecclesiastical history. It was that renowned chef, Vatel, I think, who boasted that he could cook a goat or even a rat in such an artful way that the dinner-guests would lick their fingers. I would consider it a feat if, with whatever seasoning, I have succeeded in rendering the medieval monk not savoury but merely palatable.

Before ending this long preface, perhaps I should, writing as I am in Greece, justify the license used in many parts of my book, that is, for sometimes calling things by their name instead of taking refuge in those paraphrases used by modest writers to hide their immodest meanings, just as our first parents hid their nakedness using a fig leaf. This is something I could easily have done by copying the literary theories put forward by Voltaire, Byron, Casti and others in their works. But in keeping with the French proverb, *comparaison n'est pas raison* and, what's more, I find tautology tiresome. I would simply say that I considered this license both necessary and natural to my sort of narration as salt is to the sea. Whoever has read *The Maid of Orleans* or *Don Juan* or the Italian poets of the sixteenth century will in no way condemn Joan as being overly explicit, and anyone cognizant of the middle ages who is versed in the Chronicles, Legendaries and Church Fathers, will most certainly admit that comparing the present volume with their works resembles the maiden of whom St. Basil dreamt "standing like a modest statue on her maidenhood's marble pedestal, unmoved before any fantasy or touch".

There are many, of course, who will attribute to me as the gravest of my sins the audacity with which I stir the ecclesiastical mire of the middle ages both in the West but also in Byzantium, deviating sometimes into digressions concerning the present state of our Church; yet the impartial reader of my work will be convinced of this at least; that it contains no trace of polemic. The outrages of both the Franks and the Levantines are presented with the same impassive impartiality and the visions of the medieval theologians and dreams of the German scholars are ridiculed with the same readiness. Wherever I found that I could give cause for laughter, I did so, regardless of whether it was concealed in the monastery or the university, beneath the cassock of the monk or the gown of the scholar. The religious or philosophical absurdities from the creation of the world down to our own times are presented with the same impassivity with which the mariner notes the direction of the winds in his log-book. St. Basil, Pascal and Chateaubriand championed Christianity; Libanius, Voltaire and Strauss attacked it in the name of humanity or philosophy; and they all wrote with passion and, as they themselves maintain, with deep conviction in their religious or philosophical principles. Yet whenever I read some book on a similar topic written *with purpose and conviction*, I immediately recall the words of Isidorus who writes of contemporary theologians: "Concerning matters divine and above reason they pretend to differ because they are crazed by their thirst for power"; and I admit without blushing that I had no other aim

Unless it were to be a moment merry.

Concerning my criticisms of the present-day rites of the Orthodox Church, I would say only this, that whatever people's innermost convictions may be, external worship of the Divine has everywhere and in all times been considered necessary. The simple Christian enters the church in order to find solace, hoping for the diamonds and emeralds of the Revelation of Paradise; while the scholar muses in the same place on the infinite, the ideal, the goal of man and other similar philosophical conundrums. However, the minds of both rise to concepts higher than their daily concerns and both leave those holy surroundings as better people and with a deeper comprehension of the truth of Jesus' words "Man does not live by bread alone". Yet this worship, in order to fulfill its aim, should be in accordance with people's ideas, habits and customs, which are modified daily as civilization progresses or simply changes. "The sanctum," says that most Christian apologist Chateaubriand, "must remain unchanged, but its adornments may be altered in keeping with the times". Convinced of this from long ago, the Westerners took care to exclude from their churches everything inconsistent with contemporary trends. The duration of the liturgy was limited to one quarter of an hour, the fasts are tolerable, the clergy polite, their icons are pleasing to the eye and their music charms the ear; so that without great effort or revulsion everyone is able to be a good Christian. Whereas we thought it good to remain affixed to the conventions of the middle ages, like mollusks to rocks; our liturgy, such as the one by St. Basil, lasts two hours and no one listens to it; the priests are chosen from the "scum of the earth" as in the time of St. Paul and no one heeds their counsels; the fasts are properly suited to the consequential monks and no one fasts; the icons are monstrous and no one venerates them and as for our ecclesiastical droning I consider it unnecessary to say anything here. On account of this, it follows that of all the other Christian nations, we alone, at least the progressive classes among us, are lacking not so much in faith, because this lack has come to be a more general misfortune, but rather in all form of external worship, which, as stated above, has its uses, reminding people that there are other delights apart from those of the flesh. As for me, whenever I knelt beneath the dome of some gothic church, I venerated some painting by Raphael or lent my ear to some sacred music of Mozart or Rossini, always feeling the religious sentiment being renewed in my heart and, forgetting the ecclesiastical history, I cried out like Galileo *E pur si muove*; while whoever enters one of our churches is overcome by one sentiment alone: the desire to leave. The accuracy or at least the truth of all this can only be doubted by one blind or wantonly blind. If there are among us wise men who think that we should have empty churches and illiterate and contemptuous clerics, that the nose is the most appropriate instrument for extolling the Supreme Lord, *Summer* an ethical book for young ladies and the *Confessional of Nicodemus* an appropriate handbook for priests, I too can only wait to become wise that I might partake of their opinion. Others again, though admitting that things are not as they should be, maintain nevertheless that they should remain as they are out of gratitude to the Church for liberating us from the foreign yoke and by means of which we sooner or later hope to achieve the *Great Idea*, namely, the liberation of Epirus and Thessaly. Though, in all truth, this is a rather odd kind of gratitude, for instead of healing the wounds and decorously clothing the Church that saved us, we leave it in the filthy rags of the middle ages, homeless and scorned; and all those who wish to treat it as an instrument for political ends are forgetting, it seems, that the age of miracles has long since passed, and that the sun no longer stops nor will the walls separating us from our enslaved brothers come tumbling down through the droning of our priests, like those of Jericho at the sound of Joshua's trumpets.

I have set forth all the above in order to avoid any misunderstandings and not, of course, in order to justify the book, which I submit to the mercy of the readers; as for the critics I simply remind them that it contains facts and events that are based on indisputable testimonies; so that those inclined to censure *res et non verba* should also take these to task; while those who vaguely and groundlessly protest in the name of morals, morality or moralizing or however else it may be called by our newspapers are not only unworthy of note, but in fact recall the words of the English poet, according to whom "only the immoral talk of morality".

Writ in Athens, this 1st day of January, 1866

Part 1

"Il y a bien de la difference entre rire de la religion,
et rire de ceux qui la profanent par leurs opinions
extravagantes."

(Pascal, *Lettre* XI)

It is from the middle that epic poets usually begin; the
same is true of those novelists who solicit some newspaper to refer, with "Aristotelian license",[5] to the voluminous adventures of every Porthos and Aramis as an
epic; thereupon the hero, in a cave or a palace, reclining on fragrant grass or a soft bed, avails himself of the
opportunity to narrate to his mistress all that has happened,

having had their fill of love's delights.

This is how Horace in his *Poetics* wants it; this too is
what the booksellers recommend, whenever they
commission a book, outlining to the author its length,

---

[5] See Chateaubriand, Preface to *Les Martyrs*, p.3.

breadth and material, rather like ordering a suit at the tailor's. This then is the usual way, though I prefer to begin from the beginning. Anyone who is fond of the classical disarrangement may read my last pages first and then the first, thereby transforming into an epic novel my plain and truthful tale.

Even the great Byron found the patience to listen to the idle chatter of the old women of Seville in order to learn whether the mother of his hero Don Juan recited the *Paternoster* in Latin, whether she knew Hebrew and wore a linen blouse and blue stockings. I, too, wishing to be able to tell the reader the name at least of my heroine's pater, waded through long pages of gibberish by each and every medieval Herodotus; yet I found him to have as many names and as varied as the poets have for Zeus and the Indians have for the devil. By spending years comparing manuscripts I might, perhaps, be able to learn whether Joan's father was called Willibald or Wallafrid, but I doubt very much whether the reader would thank me for all this toil. Following, therefore, the example of modern scholars, who fear lest, by wasting their time in reading, they write less themselves to the detriment both of their contemporaries and of those to come, I will return to, or rather begin, my tale.

So the anonymous father of my heroine was an English monk; from which province I was unable to learn, given that Britain was still not divided into counties for the convenience of the tax-collector. He was descended from those Greek missionaries who planted the first Holy Cross in the green valleys of Ireland and he was a pupil of John Scotus Erigena, the first to discover a method for producing ancient manuscripts, by means of which he tricked the learned men of his time, as Simonides did the Berliners. This is all that history has bequeathed to us concerning Joan's father. Her mother was called Jutha, she was fair-haired and tended the geese of a Saxon baron. Going on the eve of some feast day to choose the plumpest goose, he developed an appetite for the maid and carried her from the coop to his bedchamber. Soon becoming tired of her, he gave her to his cupbearer, who gave her to the cook, who gave her to the dish-washer, who, being a pious soul, gave the young girl to a monk in exchange for a tooth of St. Gutlhac, who lived and died a holy man in some Mercian pit. Thus Jutha fell from the bed of a noble into the arms of a monk, just as in England today the top hat has fallen from the brows of diplomats onto the heads of tramps. For in this lawful land, while many die of hunger and many provoke common decency for want of a shirt, all alike, politicians and gravediggers, earls and beggars, wear a top hat, which is considered to be the epitome of constitutional equality.

The match was a happy one. During the day the monk wandered about the surrounding castles, selling blessings and rosaries; in the evenings he returned to his cell with his hands wet from the kisses of the faithful and his sack full of bread, meats, pies and nuts; potatoes still didn't exist in England but were introduced later, together with the constitution, for the benefit of the free people, when, with the advent of equality, the servants ceased to eat choice meats from the same table as their masters.

Upon hearing the song of her returning husband far off in the valley, Jutha would set the table; that is, on some rough boards she placed a wooden platter used by both of them, an iron fork, a buffalo horn used as a cup, and stacked the fireplace with dry sticks to heat the supper. At the time, napkins, bottles and candles were known only to the bishops. After supper, the newlyweds spread sheepskins over a pile of dry leaves and lay down on the sheepskins, covering themselves with a thick wolfskin. The stronger the north wind howled outside, the thicker the snow fell, the tighter this happy couple embraced, thus proving how mistaken St. Anthony was when he maintained that the cold cools love, and so too the Greeks, who portrayed winter as an old misogynist.

Such were the days of bliss enjoyed by Joan's parents

in the joy of their fresh young limbs[6]

when one morning, while the monk was shaking the sleep from his eyelids and a strand of his wife's fair hair from his black beard, two bare-legged and barefoot Anglo-Saxon archers, carrying small shields and quivers filled with arrows on their backs, appeared at the

---

[6] Theocritus, *Idylls* 27, 67.

door of their hut, calling upon the master of the house in the name of the Heptarch Egbert to follow them and take whatever provisions they needed for a long journey. Terrified, the monk slung his pouch over his shoulders and, taking his wife in his right hand, his staff in his left and with his breviary underarm, he followed the sullen guides. Journeying on foot for three days and two nights over bare hills and moorland and, on the way, encountering many monks also being escorted by archers, they arrived, on the fourth day, at the seaside town of Garianor.[7] There was a large crowd of people gathered on the quayside, and high on a grassy elevation sat Volscius, Bishop of Eboracum,[8] blessing the faithful while a large Saxon ship was bobbing in the port, eager to hoist its mainsail to the fair wind. When the monks, sixty in number and conscripted from all parts of England, drew near, Volscius, embracing each of them one by one and handing to each two denars,[9] said to them "Go forth and teach all nations". From the Bishop's embrace, the preachers promptly stepped aboard the hollow ship and without more ado found themselves plying the murky waves of the German sea, ignorant of what shore they were sailing to in search of a martyr's crown or some grimy monastery. Yet while they are thus tossing on the sea

---

[7] The ancient name for Yarmouth.

[8] Now York.

[9] Roughly four franks.

under the protection of the Holy Cross, we would like to inform the reader what had prompted Bishop Volscius to surrender these luminaries of the English Church to the mercy of the waves. And so, to this end, bidding farewell to the British Isles, let us cross over into the land of the Franks.

Charlemagne, after wandering through Europe reaping laurels and heads with his broadsword, and after having strangled, blinded or maimed three quarters of the Saxon population, thus securing the submission and respect of the survivors, finally sought to rest on his laurels in Aix-la-Chapelle, a town famous both for its holy relics and its needles. Everything was going wonderfully well in the vast empire. Alcuin the Wise was bathing Charlemagne's dirty subjects in the holy waters of baptism, cutting their red beards and their long nails and opening up the treasure chest of his boundless wisdom to them; he rubbed the lips of one with the honey of the holy word, nourished another with the roots of grammar and taught yet another that goose quills, which make arrows fly faster, might also usefully serve as tools for writing. As for the happy Emperor, he passed his days without a care, counting his chickens' eggs, regulating his clocks and his lands, playing with his daughters and the elephant that he had received as a gift from the Caliph Aroun, sentencing murderers and robbers to a small fine and hanging from the trees of his garden those of his subjects who ate meat on Fridays or expectorated after receiving holy communion.

Yet while the pious Charlemagne, who, though not knowing how to write, did however know the ancient classics, was constantly repeating to himself:

Haec mihi Deus otia fecit,

the Saxons once again raised their insolent and unkempt heads and, plunging their hands in the blood, not of bulls, but of human victims, vowed to Teuton, Irminsul and Arminius that they would either shake off the yoke of Charlemagne or dye the banks of the Elbe and Weser with their blood. As usual, the invincible Emperor came, saw and conquered by means of the spear which, according to the Evangelists, was plunged into the Saviour's side by the Roman centurian. Indeed the Archangel Michael, appearing to Charlemagne in his sleep, placed this spear on his bed, in order to reward him, according to the chroniclers, for sleeping alone, abstaining as he was from both cooked and raw flesh during Lent. After the victory, the Holy Emperor, afraid lest he be forced once again by these savages to interrupt his pious practices, decided that all the vanquished would be put to the sword or baptized, willingly or not. No missionary ever managed to make Christians of so many infidels in so short a time; for the eloquence of the Frankish conqueror was irresistible. "Believe or die," he would say to the bound Saxon, while the executioner's blade gleamed before his eyes as the most convincing of arguments, and the entire rabble leapt into the baptismal font like ducks into puddles after the rain.

Since, however, though faith may be considered all-powerful, it is no less necessary for the Christian to know in what exactly he believes, it was common then in Europe, just as today in Tahiti and Malabar, for the newly-converted Saxons to learn a kind of catechism that was taught to them by Charlemagne's corporals, who arrayed them in rows of ten like new recruits and beat them mercilessly were they to falter when pronouncing some difficult word of the "Credo". Thus Jesus found justice for all that his early followers had suffered on account of the false idols, when they were burned by Nero or toasted by Diocletian, and from this comes the French proverb "Vengeance is the pleasure of the Gods".[10]

As long as the war lasted, the soldiers continued with their holy work; but when things quieted and the theological knowledge of these ironclad missionaries reached its limit, everyone, and above all the Emperor, felt the need for more serious catechisers. But the Franks at that time had only monks who were far better in matters of brewing than in matters of doctrine and who baptized the newborn in the name "of the Fatherland, the Daughter and the Holy Breath", who claimed that the Holy Virgin conceived through the ear, who ate before taking communion and who obliged the deacon to drink the water with which they had washed their hands after the mass. Into the hands

---

[10] *La vengeance est la plaisir des Dieux.*

of such teachers, Charlemagne did not dare entrust even the Saxons, afraid lest he be obliged before long to go to war once again to destroy new idols, namely those of Bacchus and Morpheus. At a loss what to do, he consulted Alcuin, to whom the Franks at that time went for his oracular utterances just as the ancient Greeks went to the Pythia. Alcuin was English and England then had the monopoly in theologians, just as it does today in steam-engines. So it was that a ship was sent there to be loaded with missionaries who would initiate the Saxons into the mysteries of the faith.

This saving ark of Christianity, on which we saw Joan's father embark together with his wife, was borne atop the waves for eight whole days. On the ninth, entering the estuary of the Rhine, it moored at the town of Noviomagus, where these hunters of souls first stepped onto German soil. From there, some on asses, others by boat and still others on foot like the first apostles, they made their way up to Lippspringe and finally arrived, exhausted and hungry, at Paderborn, where Charlemagne was encamped amidst crosses and shields. The conqueror promptly divided Saxony among the newly-arrived monks, each one being commanded to erect the Holy Cross in every last rural hut of this conquered land. Joan's father was commanded to head south, to Eresburg, and to pull down the idol of Irminsul, around which the revolutionaries would gather, just as our folk gather in the Hafteia district of Athens, to offer human sacrifices and each day devise new conspiracies. Our beleaguered monk, loading an ass with his wife and four loaves of black Saxon bread, set off on a new journey, pulling the beast by the bridle and, with tears in his eyes, remembering the warmth of his hut in England.

For eight whole years Joan's father wandered in the forests of Westphalia, baptizing, teaching, confessing and burying. Knowing greater suffering than even St. Paul, he was beaten many times, stoned ten times, thrown into the Rhine five times and into the Elbe twice, burned four times, hanged three times and nevertheless survived by the grace of the Holy Virgin. To any who may doubt the truth of what I say, I would refer them to the Legendaries of the time in order to read how "the fair Madonna", with "her own lilywhite arms", supported the legs of her faithful whenever they were being hanged, extinguished the flames of the fire with a fan made "of Angel's wings", whenever they were being burned, or, loosening her blue girdle, threw it to save those drowning just as Ino threw her veil to Odysseus.

All these sufferings were not enough to curb the zeal or lessen the conviction of the tireless monk; nevertheless, his body gradually became unrecogniz-able, since the Frisians gouged out his right eye, the Lombards cut off his ears, the Thuringians his nose and the savage dwellers of the Herken forest, wishing to wipe out the entire race of missionaries, sacrificed his two sons before the altar of Teuton and then, with the same inhuman blade, cut from him… all hope of fatherhood.

Even after this last misfortune, Jutha remained faithful to her mutilated husband and tried in numerous ways to alleviate his grief. Whenever, awakening in the night, he turned his one remaining eye to her in vain longing and wept for the loss of his children and his former pleasures, she would embrace him, saying: "Every day I light a candle to St. Paternus. Perhaps this patron saint of fertility will produce a miracle that we may once again know the delight of children." This wish of the goodly Jutha was soon fulfilled; not alas by some miracle on the part of St. Paternus, but by two archers belonging to the count of Erfurt. These two scallywags, encountering her on the banks of the Fulda as she was laying out in the sun the cassock of her poor husband, who, not having another one, was hiding like Odysseus in the bushes while waiting for it to dry, lay her down on the grass in similar fashion and by force reminded her of woman's earthly estate. When satiated, the two soldiers went on their way, while the hapless monk emerged from his hiding place and, putting on his still damp clothing, left that place with his distressed wife, cursing the Saxons, who in addition to his martyr's crown had now placed another kind of crown on his bald pate.

Nine months later, in the year 818, Jutha gave birth in Ingelheim or, according to some, in Mainz, to Joan, who would one day seize the keys of heaven. Her father, or rather her mother's husband, in order to accustom the newborn to the hardships of a wandering life, baptized her in the cold waters of the Mainz, in which the locals plunged their swords in order to temper the blades.

According to an old tradition, biographers have the habit of adorning the cradle of heroes with great signs foretelling their future talents. Thus, while still an infant, Hercules slew the dragon, Kriezotis a bear, bees rested on the lips of Pindar, Pascal discovered geometry at the age of ten, Byron's hero on hearing the mass in the arms of his nurse, turned his gaze from the wrinkled saints to fix them with devotion on the Magdalen, and our own heroine, destined to achieve great things in the ecclesiastical arena, would never suckle on Wednesdays or Fridays, and whenever she was offered the breast on a day of fasting would avert her eyes in horror. Holy relics, crosses and rosaries were her first playthings. Even before she cut her first teeth, she knew the Paternoster in English, Greek and Latin and, before losing her milk teeth, she was already helping her father in his apostolic work by catechising the Saxon girls of her own age. She was only eight years old when her mother, the goodly Jutha, died and, from the shoulders of the gravedigger, she delivered a funeral eulogy over her mother's grave.

And while Joan grew in beauty and wisdom, her father, exhausted from his sufferings and the loss of his wife, felt his strength growing weaker. In vain did he call upon St. Genon to steady his stumbling step, in vain did he light candles to St. Lucia, to give strength to his eye that he might distinguish the letters in the psalter, and in vain did he beseech St. Fortius to strengthen his voice. His hands trembled so greatly that one day while he was offering the Lord's body to the fair Gysla, abbess of the Bitterfeld Monastery, instead of putting the Host in the maiden's rosy mouth, he dropped it on her white breasts, which this handmaid of God kept always naked by special permission of Pope Sergius. There was a great uproar; the abbess blushed, the nuns covered their faces, the local priests cried Sacrilege! Sacrilege repeated the nuns as a faithful echo and, like maenads, leapt upon the poor old man, relieving him of his holy vestments and throwing him out of the monastery in desultory fashion.

For a full two weeks, the wretched missionary, together with Joan, wandered in the inhospitable forests between Frankfurt and Mainz, sleeping at night upon the foliage and eating mast together with the Westphalian swine. But this food, though fine for fattening up the companions of St. Anthony, soon rendered the monk and his daughter leaner than the seven ears of corn seen by the Pharaoh in his dream. In vain did the monk try to repeat the miracle of his compatriot St. Patrick, who by his supplications transformed the swine running free over the hills of Ireland into tasty hams, and in vain did he call upon the eagles flying overhead to bring him food, as St. Stephen had done—while, every so often, Joan would raise her tearful eyes to her father and cry out "I'm hungry!" At first, the compassionate father, raising his slender arms to the heavens, replied like Medea "I would open my veins that you be satiated with my blood." But gradually the hunger dried his throat and his heart so that in response to his daughter's laments, he simply said "plod on."

As the movement of a lamp led Galileo to the construction of a clock, so the hungry monk was led by a white bear to the discovery of a new way of earning a living. Seeing one of these furry polar daughters dancing at a fair and its master asking money from the spectators, he decided to exploit Joan's precocious wisdom like the beast-tamer did the bear's dancing and thus secure his daily bread and ale. Thus the wise Erasmus was right to claim that anyone with good sense might learn much even from a bear. So he began to prepare his daughter for her new profession, cramming the ten-year old girl's head with all the stuff and nonsense that the learned men of the time called Doctrine, Demonology, Scholasticism or whatever and that they wrote on parchment, from which they had erased the verses of Homer or the epigrams of Juvenal. When he considered that she was sufficiently primed for this righteous contest, he began visiting the castles and monasteries in the fertile land of Westphalia. On coming to each place, he would bow low to the lord, extol the virtues of his lady, extend his hand or the hem of his cassock to be kissed by the servants, then he would stand Joan on a table and the show would begin: "Daughter," he would ask her, "what is the tongue?"

"A whip for the air."

"And what is air?"

"The element of life."

"And what is life?"

"Pleasure for the fortunate, torment for the poor, for all the expectation of death."

"And what is death?"

"Crossing over to unknown shores."

"And what is a shore?"

"The edge of the sea."

"And what is the sea?"

"The abode of fish."

"And what are fish?"

"Delicacies for the table."

"And what is a delicacy?"

"An accomplishment of the cook."

After a sufficient time had passed of this show of knowledge in the form of question and answer on matters both theological and culinary, the father would call upon the castle's confessor to put difficult questions to the little girl from any field of human knowledge and Joan would cast the hook into the ocean of her memory and always pull out the appropriate answer, which she would base on some verse of the Holy Scripture or of St. Boniface. At the end of the questioning, she would lightly jump down from the table and gathering up the ends of her pinafore with her fingers, she would offer it as a kind of dish to each of those present, appealing to their generosity with a sweet smile. Some cast a copper coin into it, some a silver one, others eggs and yet others apples; as for those who had nothing to give, they placed a kiss on the brow of the fair-haired theologian.

They lived in this way for a further five years, eating every day and sometimes twice a day and spending the night sometimes beneath the oak beams of a noble's castle, sometimes under the thatched roof of a forest warden or a game-hunter. The years and the memories of their sufferings had tempered the zeal of the missionary, so that he no longer attempted to convert anyone who was unwilling, or baptize anyone without their consent, except, that is, for the dead that he found after some battle on the banks of the Elbe and the Rhine, for according to the prevailing opinion baptizing the dead opened the gates of heaven to them.

After so much wandering and great suffering, the old man finally crossed over to those unknown shores from which there is no return. Death found him in the cell of the good hermit Arculf, who lived a holy life beside the banks of the Main, singing praises to the saints and weaving baskets for the fishermen. After closing her father's eyes, Joan buried him, helped by the recluse, at the mouth of the river under a willow, on the trunk of which she carved an inscription recording the virtues of the dead monk. Then, collapsing onto the earth covering her only protector in the world, the wretched girl, like Othello's wife, mixed "salt tears" with the waves wetting her feet. After offering this pious libation over the paternal tomb, she wiped the tears from her eyes. The grief which we feel at the loss of a loved one resembles the extraction of a tooth; the pain is sharp but momentary. It is only the living who cause us constant pain. Who, over the grave of his beloved, has ever shed half, one hundredth, one thousandth, of the tears shed for her cruelty every day? So after Joan had finished weeping, she leaned over the water to bathe her smarting eyes. It was the first time that she had gazed with such attention at her reflection in the water, seeing the only being in the world left for her to love. Leaning too over her shoulder, let us see what was reflected in this liquid mirror. The face of a sixteen-year old, rounder than an apple, fair hair like the Magdalene's and loose like Medea's, lips crimson like a cardinal's cap and with the promise of inexhaustible pleasures, breasts as plump as a partridge, still heaving with emotion. This is how Joan saw herself in the water; and this is how I, too, saw her image in a manuscript in Cologne. This vision immediately eased the pain of my heroine, who, lying down on the grass and resting her head on her hands, began to consider how she might use her beauty and her intellect; whether she should don the habit or seek some other protector in place of her father. After musing thus for some time, overcome by the heat and dazed by the sound of the cicadas, she fell asleep in the shade of the trees, which protected her from the rays of the sun and from the gazes of the curious.

I have no knowledge of whether Joan had read Lucian, but when she closed her eyes, she too had a dream like that of the Samosatian. Two women appeared to her rising out of the water. One of them had bare breasts, flowers on her head and a smile on her lips; the other a black habit, a cross on her chest and a devout look on her face. Both were comely, but the beauty of the first recalled merry festivities, the clinking of glasses and the stepping of dancers; while the glazed look of the other recalled the mysterious pleasures of the coenobium, silent banqueting and soft kisses. The first made one want to clutch her round the waist in a boisterous dance hall, under the eyes of a multitude of spectators and the light of thousands of candles; the other to want to undo her girdle in a quiet cell in the dim light of a lamp hanging in front of the icon of some saint.

When they approached her, it was the first one who spoke: "Joan," she said, tenderly running her fingers through our heroine's fair locks, "I saw you undecided as to whether you would prefer the pleasures of the world or the quiet of the nunnery and I straightaway acted in order to lead your inexperienced steps to the path of true happiness. I am St. Ida; none of this world's pleasures escaped me; I delighted in two husbands, three lovers and seven children; I drained many bottles of fine Rhineland wine, spent many sleepless nights of pleasure; I showed my shoulders to all the world, offered my hand to every lip, let my waist be clasped by whoever knew how to dance and nevertheless I am praised and revered together with all the saints. And I enjoyed all this while eating choice fish during Lent, casting the crumbs from my table into the insatiable mouths of the priests and offering my old robes to the statues of the Virgin. Such is the future I promise to you if you heed my counsels. You are poor, homeless and in rags, but I, too, before becoming the wife of Count Egbert, had to blow on my cold fingers in winter, and my only possessions were my red lips, through which I acquired wealth, honours and sainthood. Take courage then my fair Joan. You are lovely like a flower in the meadow, wise like the book of Hincmar, wily like a fox of the Black Forest. With all this you can acquire whatever delights life has to offer. But keep to the well-worn path and leave the byways to fools. Find a husband who will give you his name and Spanish sandals, have lovers to kiss those sandals, have children to console you in your old age, also have, if you so wish, a holy cross, in which to take refuge, whenever you grow tired of the living or they grow tired of you. This is the only path that leads to happiness; the same one I followed for thirty years amidst flowers, banquets, horses and songs, surrounded by a husband who loved me, by lovers who praised my beauty and subjects who revered my name; and when the inevitable end came, I expired on a purple bed, receiving communion from the hands of the Archbishop and supported by my children. And now, without fear, I await the day of judgement beneath a marble slab, on which my virtues are inscribed in gold letters."

Thus spoke St. Ida; and such wise counsels are whispered even today by experienced mothers in their daughters' ears, inspiring in them, fortunately, revulsion for the nonsense written by the romancers. And when she had unwound the glittering rosary of worldly delights before the girl's eyes, her habit-clad companion stepped forth and, in a voice flowing sweetly, like the waters of Siloam, she began to speak:

"I, Joan, am St. Lioba, like you a child of Britain, cousin to the patron of this land, St. Boniface, and friend to your father who rests beneath its soil.

What the delights of this world are, you have heard from her. Mingling marriages, motherhood, loves, horses, she thus fashioned a gilded pill that she cast before you, like fishermen cast bait to the fish. Yet this diligent match-maker told you nothing of the cost or the defects of the merchandise. Ask her of the tears she shed when her husband rebuked her or when her lover betrayed her, how many she shed over the bed of her sick child or before the mirror when, in place of lily-whiteness and rosiness, it reflected only pallor and wrinkles. Neither fanatics nor foolish were those first maidens who, renouncing the world, sought peace under a nunnery roof. For they well knew that marriages are full of trials, having heard the cries of women giving birth or being beaten by their husbands, having seen women's bellies swollen and their breasts dripping milk and having counted the wrinkles that lined their brows from so many sleepless nights and sufferings. It was the disgusting sight of an ungirdled woman with child or giving suck that sent us to the nunneries and not the visions of angels or a taste for dry crusts, as those senile hagiographers relate. It is there that we find independence and respite in a shaded cell, in which there are no cries of children or demands of a master or cares of any kind to disturb our peace. But in order that the world may not become deserted and women rush in droves to the ceonobia, we spread bizarre rumours concerning our life, that we spend our nights kneeling on cold marble, that we water staves until they flower, that we sleep on ashes and mercilessly flog our bodies, just as forgers, in order to keep away the curious, put it about that evil phantoms and baneful spirits frequent the cave where the counterfeit coin is minted. Fear not for the *rusk* so named by St. Pachomius, which only the foolish eat, nor for the midnight bells, which wake only the gullible, nor for the poverty of our garments; see what is concealed beneath this coarse cloth."

So saying, St. Lioba threw off her habit and revealed herself clad in a gossamer garment like those made in Kos, "woven of pure air", as the poets would say, beneath which her body shone like choice wine in a bottle of Bohemian crystal. Then, whispering in the sleeping girl's ear, she continued, in an ever softer voice: "Joan, my rival here promised you pleasures, but ask her whether, surrounded by malicious eyes, she ever really felt pleasure when she surrendered to her lover, not lending her ear to his sweet words but rather to every little sound around her, turning pale and pushing him away whenever a door creaked or a leaf rustled. Have you ever seen a cat climb upon a table to drink its master's milk? Its eyes move in all directions, its ears are cocked, its fur bristles out of fear and it is ever poised ready to flee. So it is when these worldly mistresses would taste their forbidden fruits. We, however, are surrounded by neither cares nor spying eyes, but by high walls and thick groves; during the day we spend our time discussing pleasure like the ancient philosophers, yet when the hour of pleasure sounds, we retire to our quiet cells, where in silence and devotion we prepare ourselves for pleasure, as knights do for a duel. Immersing in tepid fragrances this cilice, which the foolish take to be an instrument of penance; we rub our body with it till it becomes rosy red, sensitive to every touch like a horse to the spur; we let down our hair, cover up the holy icons and, in winter, lie down by the light of a cheery fire, or, in summer, by the open window listening to the song of the nightingale or humming the Song of Songs, and thus we surrender to sweet dreams, till in the corridor are heard the sandals of the one coming to give flesh and blood to these dreams. It was the Easterners who invented twin monasteries, where the servants of the All Highest and the brides of Christ lived under the same roof, separated by a wall, but we, perfecting the invention of the Greeks, opened up holes in these walls, through which, noiselessly and without danger, we receive our Benedictine brothers. We were the first to cultivate in the nunnery gardens the aromatic rue, which frees us from the cares of motherhood, the pungent heather that renders the lips insatiable, and the stinging nettle, from which our lovers draw ever new strength, as Antaeus did from the earth.

Yet do not imagine, Joan, that our life is confined to four walls or our happiness to these pleasures.

Sometimes tedium comes in the midst of delight; the sun's course appears slow to us through the bars of our cell and the iron-clad knights seem preferable to the monks. Then, on the pretext of making a pious pilgrimage to the tomb of some saint, we go out into the world, visiting palaces and huts, theatres and spas, everywhere finding an hospitable welcome, open arms and bowed heads. When I entered the court of the Emperor Charlemagne, that very evening they were celebrating his marriage to Hildegarde. Counts, ladies, knights and prelates were crowded into the hall of the palace at Aquisgrana. The minstrels were singing of the feats of the victorious groom, the jesters and dancing girls were provoking much merriment with their strange antics, the dice were rolling and the wine flowing in silver-lipped goblets. But when I appeared in the doorway in my black habit and when my name, "Lioba, the abbess, Lioba the saint," was heard in the hall, they all abandoned their dice, their goblets and their women to turn and look at me. Some kissed the hem of my habit; others where my feet trod; only the Emperor kissed my hands. My cilice outshone the silk and the diamonds and the radiance of the powdered faces and the bare shoulders. And amidst that kneeling crowd I saw the eighteen-year old Robert who, lifting his misted eyes and joined hands to me, avidly sought my face beneath the cowl. Once the feast was over, I was led by the Emperor himself to the finest chamber in the palace that led onto the garden through a glass door. Waking at around midnight, I opened this door

to let out the smell of aloe and myrrh with which
Charlemagne's brothers had scented the room in my
honour and before me I saw Robert sitting beneath an
apple tree, with his arms resting on his knees, his
hands supporting his youthful head and with his eyes
avidly fixed on my window. When he saw me, he
jumped up in fear to run away, but with a slight nod of
my head I invited him to enter. With one bound, he
was kneeling before me, but he neither touched me nor
spoke a single word, nor did the poor youth dare even
to raise his eyes. When, parting his long hair, I touched
his brow with my lips, afraid lest he had some nightly
apparition before him, he fondled my robe, my arms
and loose hair in order to convince himself that it was
I, that he had St. Lioba, half-naked, and smiling before
him. Which of all the mistresses in the world was ever
graced by such worship and which mistresses' lips ever
plunged her lover into such an ecstasy of gratitude?

For two whole months I remained at Charlemagne's
court and when, having had my fill of banqueting,
hand-kissing and noise, I bid farewell to that hospitable palace, the Emperor himself held my ass's
bridle while the Empress and noble Ladies tearfully
implored me to remain and Robert tore at his hair in
despair. Such is the life, Joan, I promise you; pleasures
unmixed with pain in place of the dubious enjoyments
of the world, independence in place of servitude, the
staff of an abbess in place of the distaff and Jesus
in place of some mortal husband. You have heard Ida
advocating on behalf of marriage; you have heard me

on behalf of the nunnery; choose now Joan between her and me."

It was not a difficult choice, and one that was possible even with eyes closed. So, without the slightest hesitation, our sleeping heroine extended both her arms to the eloquent abbess, while her companion, defeated and unable to raise any objections, dissolved in a puff of smoke, like those demons in the guise of females who interrupted the pious study of St. Pachomius, interposing white breasts or red lips between his eyes and the breviary. St. Lioba, kissing the new proselyte's cheeks, added joyfully: "That I may be sure that your decision to embrace the monastic life is sincere, I did not tell you before what a thrice-glorious future awaits you, what a priceless reward. Semiramis became Queen of Assyria, Morgana of Britain and Bathilde of France. But see, Joan, what will become of you!"

Thereupon, a strange vision, a dream within a dream, bedazzled our heroine. It appeared that she was seated on a throne so high that her head, beneath a jewelled triple crown, was touching the clouds, while a white dove fluttered around her, fanning her with its wings and a great crowd of people on their knees was gathered at the foot of the throne. Some of these people were swinging silver incensories, the fumes from which collected around her in fragrant clouds, while others, ascending tall ladders, were piously kissing her feet.

Has it ever befallen you, dear reader, to dream that you were being hanged or that from a high place you were falling into a bottomless chasm? At the moment that the rope tightens round your neck or your body is about to be dashed, you awake and find yourself in a warm bed, with your nightcap on your head and your dog beside your feet. There is nothing sweeter than this awakening; you feel your limbs and rejoice at finding them sound, then you open wide your eyes and the window that the bad dream may not return. But if it has befallen you to have a good dream, that you found the philosopher's stone or a sensible wife, and you wake at the moment you are reaching out your arms to these chimera, then everything seems unpleasant and disgusting to you. Rejecting the tiresome reality, you bury your head under the covers, seeking in every way to grasp once again these fleeting fantasies. And this is how Joan felt when, on awakening after this delightful vision, she found herself destitute, unprotected and alone beside her father's newly-dug grave. Before long, Arculf, hospitable as ever, came to offer the orphan girl food and consolation, but she rejected both the good hermit's tasteless greens and his consolation.

"Which is the nearest monastery?" she asked him.

"The monastery of St. Blittrude in Mosbach," replied the old man in surprise, pointing eastwards with his trembling finger.

Joan thanked him and, tightening the belt on her robe, made off in the direction he had indicated, eager to acquire all the delights that St. Lioba had promised her. The pious hermit, seeing her rush off with great strides, recorded in his journal that because of all his prayers the trees giving shade to his hermitage had acquired the peculiar quality of inspiring an irresistible desire for the monastic life in whoever rested in their shade.

Joan, who in her impatience had not even thought to ask the exact way, ran like a hunted deer while the road remained straight ahead of her; but getting lost before long in narrow pathways and dead-ends, she finally halted, like Demeter, at the edge of a well in order to drink and consider what course of action she should follow. Meanwhile, the dark and moonless night was falling over the forest, and in that darkness eerily glimmering between the foliage were the eyes of owls and wolves. The unfortunate young girl, all alone in that fearful place, at times rested motionless at the root of some old oak, at others, gathering up new strength from her fear, ran between the trees like a phantom of the night. Wandering in this way, she eventually spied a faint light in the densest part of the wood and turned her weary legs in this direction, hoping to find there the hospitable cell of some hermit. But instead of this she found only a wooden statue of the Holy Virgin, positioned in the hollow of a tree, below which was burning one of those miraculous lamps, the oil in which never runs out according to the hagiographers of the times or, according to others, was daily replenished by angels. Falling on her knees before this statue, Joan prayed to the Virgin, asking for protection and a guide, that she might find her way out of that thickly-wooded labyrinth. Her prayers were heard. The braying of asses thrice responded to the young girl's supplications and, before long, the beasts appeared, sagging beneath the weight of three portly monks. They were followed by a fourth ass drawing a one-wheeled cart, on which lay two oblong boxes piously covered with silver-stitched cloth. The three mounted on the asses were friends of Joan's father, their holinesses Ralege, Legun and Regibald, who were escorting to Mulinheim the corpses of the martyred St. Peter and St. Marcellinus, between which our heroine was permitted to sit on the saintly cart. These good fathers, after listening to Joan's tale, then related to her how, at the order of their abbot Einhard, they had gone to Rome to purchase holy relics, but unable to agree on the price, they came at night, led by an angel bearing a lamp, to the crypts of St. Tiburtius' and opening the tombs of St. Peter and St. Marcellinus, who had been lain to rest there, they stole their relics, which in spite of countless dangers and hardships, they had managed to transport to Germany. At first these exhumed saints had appeared unhappy at having their peace disturbed; heart-rending sighs were heard coming from their coffins and profuse blood dripped from them each day, but gradually they submitted to their new fate and, taking up once again their old customs, they performed miracles, healing the lame, the blind and the paralytic, driving out wicked demons and changing ale into wine, ravens into doves and pagans into Christians. All this and much more was related to Joan by their holinesses, lauding the miracles of the saints as sodomists do the marvels of the Syrian goddess; but she, still with the glittering promises of St. Lioba resounding in her ears, paid little attention to her travel companions' legends of the saints, and yawning once or twice she finally fell asleep between Peter and Marcellinus. Afraid lest you have done the same, gentle reader, let us reserve for the next chapter the continuation of our truthful tale.

Part 11

"Regrettez vouz le temps où nos vieilles romances
Ouvraient leurs ailes d'or vers un monde enchanté,
Où tous nos monuments et toutes nos croyances
Portaient le manteau blanc de leur virginité?"

(Musset, *Rolla*)

Did it ever befall you, dear reader, after having spent the day reading novels about the Middle Ages, the Deeds of King Arthur or the Loves of Lancelot and Guinevere, to put down your book and, comparing those bygone times with the present, to long for that golden age, when piety, patriotism and courtly love prevailed throughout the world? When true hearts beat beneath iron breastplates and pious lips kissed the feet of the crucified Christ? When Queens wove their husbands' robes and maidens remained for long years in their castle chambers awaiting the return of their betrothed? When the renowned Roland withdrew to a cave facing the monastery guarding his beloved and spent thirty years gazing at the light from her window, while Count Robert flung himself from a high tower to save the honour of his dear princess? Often, with such memories as these, my blood flowed more warmly and my eyes filled with tears. But when, leaving aside the rhapsodists, I sought the truth beneath the dust of the centuries in the contemporary chronicles, in the laws of the kings, the "Records" of the Synods and the decrees of the Popes; when, instead of Hersart, I leafed through Baronio and Muratori and I beheld the middle ages stripped naked before me, I lamented not that this age was past, but rather that the world had never seen those golden days of faith and heroism. This book abounds in shame and ridicule, but these are the faithful, the photographic, so to speak, images of the people of those times; and I support all that I say with incontestable testimonies, just as kings support their decrees with the spear.

We left Joan journeying together with two saints, three monks and four asses. The road was dark and uneven like the style of the New School,[1] so that both men and animals were weary after two hours on those arduous paths. When they discerned from afar the red lantern of an inn on the top of a hill, they headed towards this saving light, like the magi towards the star pointing to the Saviour's manger.

From the days of Tacitus down to our own days, gluttony and drunkenness have been the characteristic mortal sin of the Germans; but while the hospitable

---

[1] Trans. note: Romantic literary movement in Greece.

inhabitants of old Germany got themselves drunk in their huts, offering supper and a roof to the weary traveller, the monks of the middle-ages, after St. Benedict had replaced wine with ale on the tables of the monasteries, frequented the taverns like the ancient Greeks the agora. In vain did the Holy Synods and Pope Leo anathematise the merchants and the imbibers of wine and in vain did the hospitable hermits build their cells on the pathways and in the woods, offering the traveller free hospitality, greens to eat and straw to lie on. The wandering clerics sometimes availed themselves of the hermits' cells when the weather was bad, but when the rain ceased, they hurried to the nearest tavern. Today, inns are constructed for the sake of the traveller; in the middle-ages many monks became travellers for the sake of the inns.

After settling the asses in the stable, the saints' relics on the innkeeper's bed and themselves in front of the fire, because summer nights were unknown in those parts, the three "holinesses" opened wide their nostrils to smell the aroma coming from the kitchen. A plump goose was turning on a spit over glowing coals and another was boiling in fine Ingelheim wine. The sight of the spit and the song of the pot gladdened the hearts of the good fathers who, sitting before long at the marble table, were already sharpening their knives and their teeth in order to rend their prey, when suddenly an upsetting recollection cast a dark cloud over the merry faces of the diners. "It's Friday!" said Ralege, pushing away the platter; "Friday!" responded

Legun, putting down his fork; "Friday!" cried Regibald, closing his open mouth, and all three gazed at
the geese like Adam at his lost paradise, despondently
biting their nails in place of the geese. The people at
the time may have been corrupt, drunkards, lecherous
and cheats, but they still hadn't succumbed like the
people of today to eating meat on days of fasting. In
Paradise in those days, just as on Olympus for the
ancients, there were patron saints of inebriation;[2]
while on earth, there were Bishops who allowed this
in accordance with the example of Ecclesiastes and St.
Augustine. But whoever failed to observe the fasts was
either struck by divine fire, like the Duke of Rocolino,
or was hanged by the Emperor's guard.

Joan, knowing all about hunger from bitter experience, pitied her hungry companions. So being well
versed in casuistry, a science unbeknown to Easterners, the objective of which was to prove black white,
the moon square and vice virtue, she searched for a
way to make it possible for them to eat without being
guilty of sin. After scratching her head for a goodly
length of time, she said to them:

"Christen the goose a fish and eat it without fear.
This is what my good father did when, captured by the
pagans, he was forced on pain of death to eat a whole
sheep on the eve of Easter. And besides, fish and fowl
were created on the same day, so their flesh is akin."

---

[2] St. Martin and St. Liutberga.

If not a good argument, it was at least well-con-
cocted. And then again, hunger which makes even dry
bread tasty, has, so it seems, the ability to strengthen
the shortcomings of an argument, at least for those
jurors who often acquit robbers on the grounds that
when they committed the crime, they had long been
hungry. For the very same reason, they should perhaps
also acquit those guilty of rape who could prove, as
Theocritus would say, that "they were in need".

Thanking Joan with a resounding kiss on the cheek,
Father Ralege picked up a glass of water and sprinkling
the geese three times said with great solemnity: "In
nomine Patris, Filii et Spiritus Sancti, hic erit hodie
nobis piscis". "Amen," responded his companions, and
before very long only the bones remained of the newly-
christened fish. After they had satiated their hunger,
the good fathers thought to quench their thirst too;
since the monks then, like the Arabs of Halima, first ate
their fill and then sought salty tidbits and wine in order
to refresh and dry their throat alternately, competing
like the dinner-guests of Mithridates as to who could
drink the most. At the time, drunkenness was the
cheapest of pleasures; a flagon of wine cost only seven
denars, so that it flowed profusely not only in the taverns but also in the churches and in the streets and in
the ladies' chambers, in no way stemmed by the decrees
of the Popes or the Synods, which were swept away by
this torrential current like trees by the flood waters. Before beginning their drinking, our "holinesses", as was
the custom then, each took the name of an angel: the

one Gabriel, the other Michael and the third Raphael, then they began emptying the drinking horns to the health, not of each other or of the emperor or of absent friends, as the commoners did, but of the Holy Virgin, of St. Peter and of all the inhabitants of Paradise. Such was required by the piety of those times, so that even this drunkenness might be rendered an act pleasing to God. Nevertheless, the night drew on, the innkeeper had gone to sleep, the oil in the lamp and the wine in the pitcher had run out and only the excitement of the monks increased with each new draught. Their eyes gleamed like those of Charon; from their mouths poured inarticulate sounds, blasphemies together with supplications to the Virgin, hymns together with Bacchic ballads. In short, the three were much the worse for wine, like Byron when he pondered over the immortality of the soul or St. Avitus when he penned the Loves of Eve. Joan, knowing well that "with wine comes debauchery and with drunkenness abuse", as Solomon wrote inveighing against debauchery in the midst of "threescore queens and fourscore concubines", quietly withdrew to the darkest corner of the room; but not even there did she find peace for very long; for the good fathers, after sating both their hunger and their thirst, felt the need to satisfy that sixth sense, for which the physicians still have found no word, while the more modest Chroniclers called it a "desire for raw flesh". Therefore, taking the hem of their cassocks between their teeth in the monastic way, they rushed upon our long-suffering heroine.

Do not be quick to blush, my gentle lady reader; the metal quill with which I write this true story is English-made, from the workshops of Smith, and for this reason modest like those fair English ladies, who, in order not to soil their immaculate dress, lift it halfway up their calves, revealing to the passers-by large feet in double-soled sandals; so there is no danger of you hearing from me what

is not becoming for a maiden to say[3]

Chased by the three monks, Joan ran around the room, leaping over tables and chairs, hurling first platters and then verses from scripture at them. But her holy eloquence and the tableware smashed in vain against these drunkards, like waves against the rocks. They were about to lay hands on her when, seeing the casks with the saints' relics lying on the bed, she took refuge behind these, like Ajax behind his shield. Their "holinesses" stepped back at first, in the face of this holy bulwark, as wolves do in the face of fire, by which shepherds protect their folds; but before long, putting aside their veneration for these holy relics, they leapt towards the bed on which the poor young girl was trembling like a lark in a hunter's net. The onset was so vehement that the bed collapsed and with it the saints' casks, from which the bones of the two martyrs tumbled to the floor. Remembering then that it was with

---

[3] Euripides, *Orestes,* l. 26.

an ass's jawbone that Samson had struck down one thousand Philistines, she prayed to the All-Highest to give strength to her right arm, then grabbing hold of one of St. Marcellinus' tibia, she too began to strike her lecherous pursuers. But it appears that their bones were stronger than those of the saint, so that before long the weapon shattered and our demure heroine exhausted all her strength and finally, after stubborn resistance, fell on the field of battle, closing her eyes resigning herself to the inevitable. But in those times there were saints in Heaven who worked miracles on behalf of maidens in distress. Just at the moment when the most holy Ralegos, who being the eldest took precedence, was bending over Joan and as the stench of his wine-soaked breath was already defiling the young girl's pale face, a huge transformation suddenly happened! An unprecedented miracle made him leap back in fear. For Joan had been transformed not into a tree like Daphne, nor into a dove like St. Gertrude, nor into a worm-eaten skeleton like Basina in the arms of Dom Rupert, but rather from her pure skin a long beard had suddenly sprouted, thick and bushy, like those covering the faces of the Byzantine saints. This is how the Holy Virgin saved maidens who were being accosted by callous monks, being ever vigilant, according to St. Jerome, just as a jealous "mother-in-law" is with the honour of her son's spouse.

Giving heartfelt thanks to the Holy Virgin for her saving intervention, Joan got to her feet and, shaking her long beard at her terrified pursuers like the head of

Medusa, left the room. Passing before the stables, she untied one of the asses and quickly mounted it to get away from that odious tavern, where she had been in danger of losing the only dowry that she had to offer to her heavenly bridegroom. It goes without saying that, the danger having passed, her beard also disappeared.

The shadows of the night and the trees of the forest gradually began to disperse. Presently, our wandering heroine found herself in the middle of a heath, having, like St. Sturm, a crystal-clear sky overhead and a black ass between her legs. Not knowing which way to go, Joan went where the pack-animal's four legs took her, but coming before long to the River Mein, she followed its meandering course, as Theseus had Ariadne's thread, till she arrived at the end of her journey as the sun was setting.

The Nunnery of Mosbach rose up at the foot of a steep mountain, where it had been situated by St. Blittrude so that the zeal of the nuns might not be cooled by the northerly breeze. Vespers were finishing at that moment and these brides of the Lord were coming out of the church holding hands and resembled a rosary of black pearls. On seeing Joan they immediately surrounded her, asking who she was, whence she had come and what she wanted. Once they learned that what she wanted was a habit, sandals and a cell, they took her to the Abbess, who betrothed our heroine to the Saviour, exempting her from the ten-month probationary period on account of the services rendered to the Church by her late father.

St. Blittrude, taking an immediate liking to the new nun because she understood the Paternoster and devoutly crossed her hands over her breast, made her curator of the convent library, which comprised sixty seven volumes; a fabulous wealth in those times. Alone from morning to night in her cell, Joan succumbed during those first days to that monastic torpor, something which besets newcomers to coenobia, like nausea does those who step aboard a ship for the first time. She came and went from her cell, cleaned the books, her nails and her hair, counted the beads on her rosary and complained to the sun for travelling too slowly to the west. Her companions were envious of the favour showed her by the Abbess and, fearing lest she pried into what they said and did, they avoided her like Brahmins do outcasts. Often, during recreation time, when the other maidens would wander in groups in the gardens happily chatting or mocking the elder nuns, relating their dreams of the previous night, showing the letters from their lovers, comparing the length of their legs and the colour of their lips and hair, Joan would remain on her own, like an obelisk in the middle of a square, measuring the height of the trees and blaming St. Lioba, because instead of pleasures she had found only boredom and tediousness in the monastery in the same way that the gold-diggers cursed the newspapers when, instead of gold, they found only rocks and fever in California.

Boredom and tediousness are, in my opinion, the chief instigators of piety. We look up to the heavens

when we have nothing to do or nothing to look forward
to on earth and we kiss the holy icons when we have
nothing else to kiss. So when Joan, who previously had
made use of her theological knowledge simply to earn
her living, learning Scripture and the Church Fathers
by heart just as Madame Ristori did with the verses of
Alfieri, found herself alone inside the four walls of her
suffocating cell, she found her present life to be empty
and began to think of the future. Truly a strange pas-
time for a seventeen-year old girl. Yet for centuries the
monasteries have been the realm of peculiar desires.
The monks in Egypt would water staves until they bore
fruit; the women saints of Hungary would eat lice and
the Hesychasts would remain for years contemplating
their navels, from which they hoped to see the light of
truth emerging. For her part, Joan, given up to metaphysical studies, would sometimes spend the entire
day poring over the writings of St. Augustine, who, as if
having witnessed them himself, described the pleasures
of the blessed and the flames of Hell and, at other times,
would run her fingers through her fair hair putting to
herself those questions concerning our present and future existence that all the inhabitants of this "vale of
tears" put to themselves in desperation, while the clerics and theologians reply with evasions and common-
places, like government ministers do when replying to
those troublesome people asking for political sinecures.
The poor girl's sleep was disturbed by strange dreams,
no longer of the goodly Lioba promising endless pleasures, but of demons shaking terrible horns or of angels

— 77 —

brandishing broadswords; sometimes she was hopeful of the joys of Heaven, at other times she was fearful of the devil's claws; one day she would believe in all the verities of Christianity from the Gospels to the miracles of St. Martin and then for three days she would be in doubt about everything; sometimes she would bow her head before the divine condemnation hanging over us and at others, if she had had any stones, she would have thrown them at the heavens to break them.[4] In short, she was possessed by that obsession which grips everyone who with sincerity seeks an answer to the problems surrounding the mystery of our existence. What are we, whence do we come, what will our fate be? Such were the questions, as insoluble in the human mind as wax is in water, that she tried to solve. Apart from all this, poor Joan's hair remained uncombed and her teeth idle; her eyes were red from lack of sleep, her face wan and her nails black. According to the renowned Pascal, this ought to be the natural state of the true Christian on earth, living constantly between the fear of Hell and the hope of redemption and, amid lamentations, seeking in the darkness the path to Paradise. Nevertheless, this state, however aristocratic it may be, however characteristic of great souls, is not one that I wish for you, my dear reader. More preferable is the cheery and carefree piety of those good Christians who, chanting hymns to the saints and eating shellfish on Fridays, un-

---

[4] The firmament was thought at that time to be of crystal.

concernedly await the pleasures of Paradise. Many are those who wish to present a superior intellect and pity these blissful mortals, but I envy the peace of their souls and the folds of their neck. If some Turk or fire-worshipper were to embrace Christianity, I would counsel him to choose above any other the Catholic church, the rites of which are so grandiose, the liturgy so short and the fasting so varied, the music so sweet to the ear and the sacred images so pleasing to the eye. As for his confessor, I would counsel him to choose not someone severe like Bossuet or Lacordaire, who would present him with a stark vision of Hell and all its inhabitants, but some sweet-tongued disciple of Escobar to lead him on a "satin carpet" to the mansions of the blessed. Since the All-Highest, according to the holy Augustine and Lactantius, "does not reject flowery paths when these lead us to Him", why should we seek Paradise among thorns and caltrops and soggy greens, listening to droning chants and kissing ugly icons? But let us return to the subject in question and let the error of my divergences be attributed to the twenty-seven Athenian newspapers and the four bells of the nearby Russian church[5] that are constantly interrupting the thread of my narration.

Grave maladies, plague, smallpox, love and the afflictions it brings and which share the same name as its

---

[5] Trans. note: Roïdes lived in Athens in Philhellenon Street where a Russian church is situated.

fair mother have this one good thing in common; that we only succumb to them once. Of such a sort was Joan's metaphysical affliction. After having spent three months scratching her head, seeking a solution to the insolvable conundrum, she finally closed her books and, opening the window in her cell, smelled the fragrances of spring. It was almost the end of April and nature, verdant, smiling and sweet-smelling, resembled a young girl decked out by an experienced maid. The vernal scents intoxicated the young nun who, having been three months in the darkness of her cell and of metaphysics, gazed at and imbibed even more insatiably the meadow grass and the smell of the violets. Between the spring and our hearts when we are twenty years' old, there is, according to both the poets and the doctors, a mysterious and inexplicable relationship, like that of Socrates with Alcibiades. Whenever we see trees in leaf, soft grass or shady caves, we immediately feel the need for an Eve in this earthly paradise. During the hours of his musing, Nero desired that the entire human race should have one head, so that he might sever it. Has it never happened to you, dear reader, while sitting in spring in the shade of a pine or rosebush, to wish that all the women in the world had only one mouth in order to kiss them all? Feeling her breast rising and falling like waves on the sea, Joan recalled the dream and the hopes that had filled her when she had come to that monastery, where she had found only tedium, old books and disturbing thoughts. "Lioba! Lioba! When are you going to fulfill your promises?" she cried out, shaking the bars of her prison in desperation. But the bars were of iron while the hands of the young nun had, through lack of work, become white and soft like the wax of candles; so leaving them and not having in her cell even a dog to beat or Chinese vases to smash, she buried her face in her hands and began to weep. There is nothing sweeter than tears, when there is a hand ready to wipe them away or lips willing to imbibe that "rain of the heart", as the Indians call them. But when one weeps alone, tears are then real and bitter, like every reality in the world; and even more bitter when we grieve not for the loss of something on earth, but because we are unable to enjoy the object that we covet, whether it be a horse, a ministry or a woman.

Presently, the sound of footsteps in the corridor distracted Joan from these sad musings. The door opened and in walked the Abbess holding by the hand a still beardless youth wearing the characteristic robes of St. Benedict and with his gaze fixed on his sandals out of modesty. "Joan," said the Mother Superior, presenting the young monk to our bewildered heroine, "the Abbott of Fulda, St. Rabanus Maurus, intends to send missionaries to Thuringia and has asked me to prepare for him the Epistles of St. Paul written out in gilt letters on fine parchment, so that the glitter of the gold might dazzle the eyes of the pagans, thereby inspiring in them greater respect for the truths of the Gospels. This young Benedictine here is Father Frumentius, outstanding like you in both piety and

calligraphy. Work with him until you have carried out
the request of our brother Rabanus. Procure for yourself some gold-leaf ink; you have pens. I will have food
sent to you from my own table. Farewell, my children."
So saying, St. Blittrude left, closing the door behind
her, like the peasants do in Moldavia when the local
Lord visits their wives. But St. Blittrude was one of
those virtuous women for whom it is impossible to
suppose anything bad. If she saw a monk kissing one
of the maidens in the nunnery, she wanted to believe
that he was doing it in order to bless her. Stricken in
childhood with smallpox, she had known only innocent kisses and thus it was impossible for her to believe
that there could be any other kind in the world. Besides, in that age, the followers of St. Benedict, men
and women, lived all together in the monasteries, like
leeches in a jar of water. According to some chroniclers, the relationships between them were innocent
like those of our own St. Amoun, who for eighteen
whole years slept together with his wife and yet she
died a virgin. According to Muratori, however, this
communal living bred many scandals and children.
But the latter were usually cast into the river of Fulda.
In this way the honour of the Monastery was preserved
and the fish grew fatter.

When alone and knowing how precious time was,
the young pair rolled up the sleeves of their robes and
immediately set to work, copying, that is, the Epistles
of St. Paul. Every morning for two weeks the young
monk would come to Joan's cell, where they worked

together till evening. Yet this eighteen-year old boy, who since childhood had been a copier of prayers but who had never read the Scriptures or the Confessions of St. Augustine or even St. Basil's Discourse on Virginity or any other holy book, was therefore as pure and unsullied as the snow in which St. Francis rolled in order to overcome the temptations of the flesh. Consequently, while the copying of Paul's Epistles progressed speedily, his relations with Joan remained at a standstill. Whenever our heroine's hand touched his hand or their hair became entangled as they pored over the parchment, he felt his heart pounding like the bells of a fortress sounding the alarm, but not even he could say whether it was pounding on the right or on the left. For her part, Joan, having many times read Origen, Chrysostom and the Rules of Nesteutes, knew everything in theory and could discuss these matters using those technical terms which are known only to doctors, whores and theologians. But it was the first time she had ever found herself alone with a man and her consternation increased daily, like that of the English travellers in the Egyptian necropolises that they had studied so meticulously on paper.

In fact, the situation of the young couple grew more unbearable each day. Frumentius didn't know what to ask for and Joan didn't know what to give. Nevertheless, their work of copying was coming to an end; the only thing left was the Epistle to the Hebrews and then the bitter and inevitable separation would come. Like another Penelope, Joan would erase at night what they had written the previous day. Her companion was aware of the ruse, guessed the reason for it and blushed or let out sighs capable of turning the sails of a windmill. Yet he confined himself to this and each day followed the next, full of vain longings and dashed hopes. But neither you, dear reader, nor I, have so many days to lose. Moreover, in writing a true tale, I am unable to imitate the poets or those writers who, loading up palpitations, tears, blushes and other Platonic provisions, couple together their mellifluous verses, like farmers do oxen to the plough, or hone their sentences, making them smooth like the breasts of Aphrodite. The great Dante referred to such writers as "procurers", but I like neither the name nor the practice. So leaving all this to Plato, Ovid, Petrarch and their tearful followers, I will present the truth naked and unkempt as when it emerged from the well.

The amorous couple had finished copying the last of the saint's Epistles, while the sun, which Galileo had not yet rendered stationary, followed its daily course. It was the hour that the oxen return to their stable and Christians kneel before the Holy Virgin reciting the "Hail Mary". The bell had called the nuns to vespers and no noise was now to be heard in the corridors of the nunnery. Joan was sitting beside the window leafing through a book of Holy Scripture, while Frumentius was gazing rapturously at his companion, whom the setting sun, coming through the cell's red windows, had crowned with a radiant light, like the Russian iconographers do the heads of the saints. Our heroine, seventeen-years old at the time, did not resemble those pallid and angelic-looking maidens that one does not dare to touch, afraid lest they open their wings, nor could she be compared to a rosebud but rather to that plant found in the warm clime of Palestine which on its branches offers the hungry wayfarer not only fragrant blossom but also tasty fruit. The shade of the cell and the nunnery's good food had firmed the flesh and softened the skin of our heroine, while her hair, having only been cut once, flowed thicker than ever before over her rounded shoulders. In truth it was always unkempt, uncombed and uncared-for, but as the poet[6] says: "gold needs no gilding, roses no extra scent, nor lilies a rosy hue," nor, in my opinion, does a seventeen-year old girl need perfumes or tresses.

Frumentius continued to keep silent and Joan to turn the pages of the Holy Book, sometimes whispering between her teeth, sometimes reading the verse out loud. But presently she ceased to turn the pages and in the mellifluous voice of a young Indian girl charming a venomous snake, she began to read:

"The song of songs, which is Solomon's. Let him kiss me with the kisses of his mouth. How much better is thy love than wine and the smell of thine ointments than all spices! Thy name is as ointment poured forth, therefore do the virgins love thee. Behold thou art fair, my beloved, and pleasant in our bed chamber. My

---

[6] Shakespeare.

lord shall lie all night betwixt my breasts. Come my beloved, let us go forth into the field; and there I will give thee my loves. Stay me with flagons, comfort me with apples; for I am sick from love. Set me as a seal upon thine heart, as a seal upon thine arm: for love is strong as death. Many waters cannot quench love, neither can the floods drown it."

On hearing all this and not knowing that the apples, breasts and kisses were religious allegories depicting the Saviour's future love for his Church, Frumentius felt his flesh and hair tingling with desire like Job's did with fear. With each verse of that heavenly canticle, he took one step nearer to the girl, and by the last verse he was down on his knees before her. Then Joan lifted her head up from the book and the gazes of these two lovers met. Whenever one finds oneself on a cliff edge (and this, I presume, was the position of our heroine), one should, so they say, close one's eyes, otherwise one grows dizzy and falls. But she did not close her eyes, so that… the book fell from her hands and

Quel giorno più non vi leggero avanti .[7]

During the peace following the Crimean war, the Prussian emissary asked for an eagle's feather in order to write his name and his titles on the treaty; would that I had a feather from the wings of Cupid in order

---

[7] Dante, *Inferno*, canticle V.

to describe the new couple's ephemeral bliss. Solitude, quiet, abundant food, spring breezes; they lacked nothing of those things that render lovers content. Excused from matins, studies, devotions and other monastic chores on account of the copying, Joan was able to remain with her companion from morn to night. Yet, though it was the middle of June, the days still seemed short to their insatiable young lips. Often, during vespers, sitting together beside the open window while the bells tolled mournfully as if lamenting the dying day, they too sighed and, like Joshua, cried "Halt" to the sun; but it continued its course to bring light to the antipodes while our lovers waited for the next day.

Ten more days passed inside that narrow cell, writing, eating, kissing, and their time spent together, which was beautiful, had no other blemish than that it passed too quickly. But eventually the dreaded day of their separation dawned. The copy of Paul's Epistles had finished long before and the abbot had sent Frumentius a mule and strict orders to return to the fold. The wretched young man, cursing his vows, his superior and all the saints went to bid farewell to his companion, holding his wayfarer's staff, but he was unable to hold back his tears. Joan did not cry because some of her fellow nuns were present; for women, however sensitive they may be, cry only when and where it is necessary. If you doubt this, dear reader, ask the ships' captains and ask history. The Empress Judith received her husband with a smile after the hapless Robert had plunged from a window in order to save her; Queen Margot laughed in order to avert any suspicion while, on her account, Boniface was beheaded before her; and the countess Carousi tightly embraced her lord, bloodstained as he was from the murder of her faithful friend. The chroniclers lauded the bravery of these forbearing ladies, but I never admired these heroines nor the sensitivity of those fragile English women who, on their way to listen to Ristori, noted in the margins of *Myrrha* and *Medea* where they should cry.

But when Joan was once again alone, she felt in the pit of her stomach that leaden weight which afflicts us when we overeat or lose our mother, lover or our fortune. According to the wise Plutarch, not even the shadow of true love is known to women; I, for my part, believe that for them it is some parasitic illness, born from boredom and loneliness, as lice from filth. Worldly women, moving from the arms of one man to the next each evening (at the ball I mean), have no time either to breathe a sigh or to love anything other than their fan. They resemble the ass that remained hungry amid four piles of trefoil not knowing which to choose first. Perhaps I am mistaken, but all the lovesick women I have met were either recluses or young girls guarded by their vigilant parents like the apples of the Hesperides or over-ripe ladies numbering more years than teeth. The despondency of poor Joan, alone inside those four walls, where during the previous days so many kisses and vows of love had resounded, increased with every day. Whenever St. Augustine grew melancholic, he "rolled in the dirt as in a scented bath"; St. Genevieve wept till she was obliged to change her blouse; St. Francis embraced snow-covered statues; St. Libania tore at her flesh with a metal comb and St. Liutberga drowned rats. Wiser than all these, our own heroine sank into a corner of her cell and using a fan made of dove feathers (the only ones allowed in nunneries) attempted to drive away the flies and her troubling thoughts. The heat of June rendered her sorrow even more burning, while the days seemed as long to her as do the days of some aged uncle to his heirs. At the height of her desperation and in order to escape the troubling phantoms surrounding her, she would sometimes seek refuge in the pious counsels of the Legendaries or sometimes whip herself with the cord of her cassock or soak her bed sheets with cold water or try to drown her sorrows in wine in keeping with the advice of Ecclesiastes.[8] But always these wondrous antidotes would fail to dispel her despondency, even that *agnus castus*, the smell alone of which is sufficient according to the hagiographers to drive away love just as pyrethrum does fleas.

Time, they say, heals all wounds; but not, I believe, those of love or hunger. On the contrary, the more one exercises restraint or fasts, the more his appetite

---

[8] "Offer to the sorrowful intoxication and to the grieving wine to drink."

increases till he ends by eating his shoes, as Napoleon's soldiers did in Russia, or by becoming amorous with his goats as the shepherds in the Pyrenees. It was in this state more or less that our heroine found herself when, one evening, while sitting on the edge of the fish pond despondently sharing her supper with the carp, the nunnery gardener mysteriously approached her and, glancing nervously round about him, like a fox about to enter a hen coop, mysteriously handed her a letter written in red ink on the fine skin of a still-born lamb. On unfolding it, amidst the flowery garlands, broken hearts, kissing doves, flaming candles and other passionate symbols with which lovers then used to adorn their letters, like our own sailors do their arms and legs, Joan read the following:

FRUMENTIUS TO HIS SISTER JOAN
REJOICING IN THE ALL-HIGHEST

"As the hart panteth after the water-brooks so panteth my soul after thee, my sister.[9] Take up a wailing for me that my eyelids gush out with waters.[10] My tears are the food of the day and the sleep of the night.[11] The hungry dream of bread but I saw thee asleep, Joan, yet waking found thee not beside me.[12] Going up then

---

[9] Psalm 41, 2.

[10] Jeremiah 9, 18.

[11] Psalm 79, 6.

[12] Isaiah 29, 8.

to my black ass I approached thy holy tabernacle. By the grave of St. Bona I await thee. Come my love, chosen of the sun, come with thy rays overshadowing the moon."[13]

Such was Frumentius' letter. When writing to a woman today, we borrow from Foscolo and Sand, but lovers then copied from the Psalms and the Prophets so that their letters were burning like the lips of the Sunamite and the sands of the desert.

At around the fifth hour of the night, when the bell called the maidens to matins, Joan, holding her sandals in her right hand and her heart in her left in order to soften its pounding, descended the stairs of the nunnery, creeping silently like a snake in the grass. The moon, that faithful lamp for smugglers and adulterers, which the poets euphemistically called "chaste" just as they called the Furies "modest", having risen behind the monastery rampart, lit the way for our fugitive heroine, who hastened to the meeting, heartlessly trampling over the cucumbers and leeks in the nunnery garden. After walking like this for roughly half an hour, she eventually arrived at the graveyard which was surrounded by cypresses and oaks so thick that not even a breath of wind or a ray of sunlight could penetrate that gloomy refectory for worms. Frumentius had tied his ass to a tree shading St. Bona's

---

[13] Song of Songs 1, 5.

tomb on which he was sitting holding his staff with a horn lantern attached and using it as a beacon for his beloved. When he saw Joan timidly approaching between the graves, he rushed towards her like a Capuchin monk towards a side of ham at the end of Lent. But the place was not suitable for such effusions; so hanging the lantern from the ass's neck and jumping on its back together with Joan, he hastened to get away from those gloomy shadows. The poor beast, sagging under its double load but also spurred on by the prodding of four heels, closed its long ears and broke into a run, emitting in a form of protest such deafening brays that (according to one reliable hagiographer) many of the maidens at rest there, believing that the final judgement had come, raised their hairless heads from the graves.

With her arms around the chest of the goodly Frumentius for support, Joan inhaled the air of the countryside with indescribable joy. Having emerged from the forest, the young couple were already riding over an open plain sown with barley and beans. Before very long the sun began to rise and, in order to protect his companion from the summer rays, the young monk, by means of a miraculous invocation, obliged a large eagle to open its wings over her head and to follow the course of the ass. Such were the miracles performed at that time by Christians, whose hearts were pure, whose faith was strong and whose prayers to the Holy Virgin were powerful, whereas today the erudite but disbelieving savants of the century, holding compasses and microscopes rather than crosses and rosaries, knowing how many feathers each bird has in its tail and how many seeds are contained in the calyx of every flower, are nevertheless unable with a simple nod to tame eagles or with one tear to transform thorns into lilies. And in addition they are cursed by his holiness the Abbot Gerinus, who calls them idolaters because they keep Mercury and Venus[14] in the Christian heavens and atheists because they alter the names of plants, crying like another Jeremiah "Anathema! Anathema! And thrice anathema on all progress and science."

After journeying for four hours, the fugitives stopped to rest beside a small lake, on the shore of which had once stood a giant statue of Irminsul. The idol had been toppled by a breath of St. Boniface and consigned to the bottom of the lake; but its old worshippers, though now having become Christians, maintained in their innermost hearts remnants of devotion to their now drowned protector, to whom they continued to offer gifts, every year casting into the water pies, candles, honey cakes and cheeses to the great delight of the fish which, because of these offerings, had become as fat as the priests of Rhea or of the Madonna of Loreto. Frumentius, who was descended on his mother's side from the heroic warriors of Witikend, was nevertheless superstitious like any true

---

[14] The planets, that is.

scion of Saxony, while Joan, though a clever theologian, shared like Socrates the superstitions of her contemporaries. Most of the Christians of that time, still vacillating between Christ and the idols, resembled that pious old woman in Chios, who would every day light a candle to St. George and another one to the Devil, saying that it was good to have friends everywhere. So our two lovers, kneeling down on the lakeshore, offered to Irminsul the remains of their breakfast and some hair from their heads mixed with a few drops of blood, thereby rendering their union eternal and unbreakable like that between the Doge of Venice and the sea. Following the ceremony, Frumentius took a monk's cassock from out of his bag and asked his beloved companion to put it on so that she might be accepted as a novice in the Monastery of Fulda. "In that way," added the young lad blushing, "we will be able to share the same cell undisturbed, eating from the same platter and dipping our pen into the same inkpot, whereas if they see you to be a woman, the elders will want to confine you with the other female novices in the women's quarters, which only they are allowed to enter, and I shall die of despair on the doorstep."

Refusing to disguise herself as being an act of impiety, Joan countered her lover's entreaties with a verse from Scripture: "The woman shall not wear that which pertaineth unto a man, neither shall a man put on a woman's garment," but he insisted and responded to the verse from Deuteronomy with the views of Origen, according to which women will be transformed into men on the day of judgement. When Joan replied saying that Origen was a heretic and a eunuch to boot, the young lad reminded her of the example of St. Thecla, the sister of St. Paul, and, in addition, of St. Margaret, St. Eugenia, St. Matrona and so many other women saints, who, concealing their body, "white like an angel's wing", beneath a man's robe, attained sainthood while living together with monks, rather like Turks who attain paradise while living among women. His youth, comeliness and passion were arguments that rendered the young preacher's eloquence invincible so that, before very long, trampling on the injunctions of Scripture and on her woman's robe, Joan donned the cassock and wore the sandals which, after some years, she would extend that they might be kissed by the world's mighty as they knelt before her throne. Once the transformation was complete, Frumentius led her to the edge of the lake that she might gaze upon her reflection. Never had a cord tightened round the waist of a more comely monk; our heroine's face shone beneath her monk's cowl like a pearl inside an oyster. Frumentius could not have his fill of marvelling at his brother "John", before whom, kneeling as in ecstasy, he began to laud his fellow-monk's beauty by means of those mystic-anatomical hymns with which the monks in the middle ages extolled one by one the body parts of the Holy Virgin, her hair, her cheeks, her breasts, her belly, her legs and her feet, as horse-dealers do the beauty of their horses and Mr P. Soutsos[15] that of his heroines.

When the litany was over, the young couple again mounted the pack-animal and directed its steps towards the Monastery of Fulda, where Joan would be inducted into the fold of St. Benedict. It took the fugitives twelve whole days to cover the thirty leagues between Mosbach and Fulda, resting wherever they found shelter, bathing in the streams and carving their names on the trees that shaded their pleasures. The heat of the sun, of youth, of love and, above all, of the journey by ass rendered these frequent stops necessary. Besides, knowing precisely the saintly topography of those places, Frumentius would always find some pious reason whenever he wanted them to get down, whether it was to pray before the tree where St. Thecla healed a blind man by sprinkling his eyes with drops of milk from her virginal breasts, or to kiss the ground where St. Boniface's blood had flowed and from each drop of which an anemone had blossomed, as with Adonis. Smiling, Joan consented to her lover's requests, while the shepherds and farmers admired both the beauty and the piety of the two cowled youngsters, rushing whenever they encountered them to remove their three-cornered hats and vying with each other as to who would be the first to kiss their

---

[15] Trans. note: Panagiotis Soutsos was a romantic writer and poet belonging to the First Athenian School and a contemporary of the author.

hands or to offer them bread, goat's cheese, ale and fruit. At other times, they encountered half-naked Slavs, who lived like reeds on the riverbank, demanding tolls from wayfarers and throwing those who refused into the water. But Frumentius drove them away with a hymn to St. Michael, so that these amphibious robbers were immediately put to flight as elephants are by a pig's squealing. Then one morning while, in the shade of an old oak tree, the happy couple were resting on their amorous laurels or rather on trefoil (as laurels in Germany grow only on the heads of heroes), two women appeared, their legs bound together with a light chain, their cheeks rouged and with nothing to cover them save their long flowing hair. They were sinful women, ordered by their confessor to go, naked and fettered, to venerate the tomb of St. Marcellinus in order to atone for their sins. Pious excursions of the sort usually took place at the end of spring or the start of summer when the temperature allowed such paradisiacal attire. Most of these Magdalenes, knowing that the touch of the holy relics would quickly cleanse them of every stain, were in no way averse to multiplying their sins on the way, seeking hospitality from the peasants and alms from wayfarers and rewarding both with that same coin by which St. Mary of Egypt paid her passage, while their *au naturel* attire naturally facilitated such transactions. So these two pilgrims, incapable of guessing what was concealed beneath Joan's cassock, came up to them asking for a few denars, in return for which they promised to open the gates of paradise to the young couple in the life hereafter and to open their arms in the life here and now. Having Joan in front of him as a breastplate shielding him from all temptation, Frumentius used the cord from around his waist to fend off the shameless propositions of the two unrobed sirens, from whom he turned, clutching his beloved to him like ascetics do the cross whenever they are tempted by the demons of the flesh. Yet these saintly hermits, while fearfully turning one eye from the demon, fix the other on it with desire and also horror, like a hungry Jew on a side of ham; Frumentius, on the other hand, as a true child of the west, using pleasure as an antidote against dèsire, effortlessly averted both his eyes. Our own saints would keep vigils, castigate themselves and fast till their mouths filled with worms and yet only barely managed to placate the screaming flesh, struggling night and day against devils disguised in female form and driving fowl and she-goats away from the hermitage as being dangerous to their unbearable continence; whereas the Franks, making a small sacrifice to quell the onset of lust, are then able tranquilly and with peace of soul to tend to their redemption, no longer forced to interrupt their prayers every so often in order, like St. Anthony, to drive away their temptation by means of a cold bath. According to the wise Archigenes, continence is the most powerful of aphrodisiacs; so the Franks were quite right to ban such practices from their monasteries.

The sun, having given its light to the longest day of the year, had long since set when our two wayfarers, passing the two dormant volcanoes surrounding the Monastery of Fulda, finally set foot on monastery land. The night was moonless and balmy and only the stars could be seen reflected in the stream of Fulda; but as the youngsters were approaching the monastery, they discerned between the trees a red glow like that of a large fire. Foxes, deer and huge wild boar were running all around them in terror, while the night birds flying in confusion above them were seeking their shaded nests. Trembling, Joan tightened her arms around her lover's chest, while the ass cocked its ears in alarm, proceeding cautiously and furtively like one of the Pope's soldiers into the fire of battle. Columns of flame, clouds of smoke, the sound of bells and chanting, the smell of incense and cooking soon assailed the eyes, ears and nose of our heroine, whose wonderment and fear increased at every step, nor was she at all reassured by the apparent jollity of Frumentius, who to her endless questions replied with chuckles and kisses. Unable to answer you, gentle reader, in similar fashion, we should inform you that this particular day or rather night was the twenty-fourth of June, on which day eight hundred years previously, the head of St. John had been offered to the daughter of Herodias as a reward for her dancing, just as today a bouquet of flowers is offered to Esler or Taglione. The saint's bones, disinterred by St. Athanasius, were carried throughout the world, as was the custom then, working their miracles; while the head had been taken by a French monk from Alexandria to France, because the Franks of the middle ages would snatch from the Eastern Church the relics of saints like their descendants do the remnants of ancient art. A finger of St. Sergius or a tibia of St. Febronia fetched a far higher price then than a head of Hermes or an arm of Aphrodite does today. The head of St. John was placed in the Abbey of St. Jean d'Angély and used by the local inhabitants as a cure for fever just as quinine is used today. The fame of this miraculous head gradually spread throughout the west and every year, in honour of the saint, numerous bonfires were everywhere lit, around which the faithful danced and revelled, as their ancestors had around the torches of the Parilia. The goddess Pales had been long forgotten, but her old worshippers continued to love wine, dancing and all-night revels and, for lack of gods, offered to the bearded and robed saints of the Christian paradise the joyful worship of the naked and beardless inhabitants of Olympus.

The festivity was at its height when the two wayfarers entered the Monastery courtyard. Some of the monks were adding bales of straw and empty barrels to the fire, while others, lifting the hem of their cassocks, were leaping over the sacred flames and finishing up in a pool of water whenever the fire singed their bare legs; others were dancing around the fire, like David around the ark of the covenant or were lying on the grass, dipping their forks into the pots and their cups into the pitchers; still others, holding flaming torches, were running around the garden looking for hieracium in order to drive away demons, or four-

leafed clovers, which render the infernal spirits subject
to whoever finds the plant on this particular night.
With cries of joy the merry monks welcomed their
returning brother and Joan, whom he presented to
them as an orphaned relative who had been a vassal
of the Duke Ansegisus and who, finding the chains of
bondage to be heavy, wished to exchange them for the
monk's cord. "Dignus, Dignus est intrare in nostro
Sancto Corpori!" the Benedictines replied in unison,
pulling the neophyte into the whirl of their circular
dance, which twisted and turned like a long serpent
round the largest of the fires. Joan, on first entering the
monastery, had to learn to dance. For, in those times,
dancing, forbidden today by the clergy as being the
work of the Devil, was in no way considered impious
or sacrilegious, but was simply a prayer performed
by the feet like psalms are by the lips, and both were
invented by King David, which is why they are closely
related like true children of this same father.

The stars were fading in the heavens and the fires
dying out on the earth below when the bell obliged the
inebriated and sleepy drinking companions to leave
the dance and the pitcher and hasten to matins. That
morning, as always happened on the day following
a feast, instead of hymns, loud snoring resounded
beneath the domes of the church and, for this reason,
so it is said, the monks had retained the habit of chanting through their noses even when awake. This custom, banished by the churches in the west along with
the Feast of the Ass and the other medieval gothic

remnants, came down to us, where it is still preserved and indeed flourishes, rendering the churches emptier by the day and the piety and charity of the Orthodox less fervent and forthcoming. Religions are rather like women. Both, when youthful, require neither adornments nor cosmetics in order to be surrounded by worshipful devotees, ready even to lay down their lives for them, as did the first Christians and the lovers of Aspasia; but when they age, they are obliged to have recourse to powders and jewellery in order to keep their dwindling adherents a little longer. The Roman Church, realising this upon seeing the diminishing zeal of its faithful, had recourse to artists and sculptors, as Hera did to Aphrodite's veil in order to hide her wrinkles and garb her nakedness; while the Eastern Church, though older than its sister church, either out of poverty or pride, continued to want to attract its faithful by means of nasal chanting and scowling icons. Devotion vanished long ago from the world, but the paintings of Raphael or the voice of Lacordaire or of the Pope's castrati continued to draw worshippers beneath the domes of St. Peter's and the Pantheon, whereas we only go to church once a year and plug our ears.

When the matins were over, Frumentius hastened to show Joan around her new confines. The Monastery of Fulda was more like a fortress than a haven for monks. High volcanoes, the smouldering craters of which had been extinguished by St. Sturm with a few drops of holy water, surrounded it on all sides, while the stream of Fulda served as a moat for this fortress topped by turrets and serrated ramparts. The then followers of St. Benedict liked, apart from wine and sleep, to involve themselves in the political arena of the time and whenever they were being hounded by some powerful adversary, they would barricade themselves behind the walls of the coenobium just like the newspaper reporters do behind the articles of the Constitution. And though Charlemagne had tempered the tendencies of the bellicose monks, depriving them of all but spiritual weapons, the monasteries still maintained their warlike appearance. Joan visited one after the other the cells, the novices' study room, the refectory decorated with monstrous statues of the twelve apostles, the underground dungeons, in which the bad monks were buried alive and, finally, the library, where sixty scribes worked night and day; some erasing ancient manuscripts and others recording on the parchment thus prepared the lives of St. Babylas and St. Prisca in place of the labours of Hercules or the feats of Hannibal. The garden was overrun because the good fathers had little care for flowers and detested vegetables because they took up valuable space in the stomach, preferring the breasts of geese and the loins of swine and likening these to the sayings of Scripture, which, though short, contain great substance.

Having described this abode, we will now endeavour to present a picture of its inhabitants. The Monastic Orders had so multiplied and there had appeared such a variety of names and apparel for the monks:

Theatines, Recolletti, Carmelites, Johannines, Fransiscans, Cappuchins, Camaldolese, the barefoot, the sandalled, the bearded, the shaven, the white-robed, the black-robed and more, so that the renowned Baron Boru, in order to avoid confusion, attempted to categorise them according to their chief features of genus and type in keeping with the system used by Linnaeus for plants and animals. So, opening this "Linnaean Monachologia" at the word "Benedictine", we read the following scholarly definition of this type of cleric: "...shaven face, tonsured head, sandalled feet; wears a long black cassock, a cloak down to the heels... caws three or four times each day and at night in a slow, rasping voice... eats everything, rarely fasts."

These were the main characteristics, but, in addition, the German Benedictines wore a picture of the Holy Virgin sewn onto their cowls to protect their heads from evil thoughts and from lice. Their faces greatly resembled the palimpsests of monastic manuscripts, on which were still visible, beneath the pious hymns of the middle ages, the love verses of Anacreon and Sappho. These holy fathers ate four times each day; instead of butter, they used pork dripping and instead of forks they used their fingers, while sinners were punished by being deprived of the dripping for some weeks as we are deprived of receiving the Holy Eucharist. They shaved twice a month, while on Good Friday they all washed their feet and three times a year the more portly of them submitted themselves to blood-letting in order to placate their impure desires or, according to some chroniclers, in order to prevent apoplexy. The majority were illiterate, though some knew the *Paternoster* and others knew how to write. Like Homeric heroes, these latter were given a double portion at table and wine instead of ale. They all of them honoured the Sabbath, and because it is not known precisely on which day God rested after having finished creating the world, and afraid lest they made an error, they remained idle throughout the whole week. Finally, the constitution of these monks was so robust that most of them died on their feet, like Russian soldiers, whom, so it is said, have to be pushed after death in order for them to fall to the ground.

The shepherd of this cowled flock was at the time the renowned St. Rabanus Maurus, whose memory had more drawers in it than an apothecary's workshop. The wise abbot, having crossed all the seas on which travellers had ever vomited, had a command of every living and dead language and, in addition, had a knowledge of Astrology, Magic, Canon Law and Midwifery, actually having invented an apparatus by means of which embryonic Christians could be baptized in their mother's womb, so that, in cases of miscarriage, they might avoid the dark realms where unbaptised children wander, as unburied pagans do on the banks of the Styx. When Joan entered the Monastery of Fulda, St. Rabanus, already aged and suffering from dyspepsia, was more concerned with his own salvation, eating only greens, like Nebuchadnezzar during the last years of his life, when, that is, he was transformed into a bull, and composing hymns to the Holy Cross. Each of these hymns consisted of thirty lines and each line of an equal number of letters arranged in the form of a cross, like the Bacchic odes of the French poets that were in the form of a bottle or a barrel. Copying out these masterpieces required an experienced calligrapher and in this there was no one able to compete with Frumentius and the new brother "John". So it was to them that the cassocked hymnodist entrusted his poetic crosses that Frumentius' prophecy might be fulfilled concerning the two of them: "dipping their pens into the same inkpot".

The happy lovers resembled those fortunate peoples who have no history. The life of our monks flowed smoothly and peacefully in the shade of the monastery, like the stream of Fulda under the shady old poplars. Have you ever considered, dear reader, how pleasant and restful it would be to have a lover in men's attire and who revealed her charms to you alone? You would not know jealousy or any of those countless thorns which, according to St. Basil, render women "a workshop of sorrows". Her men's clothes would protect her more securely than the keys to the Turkish harems and those chastity belts by which the Italians secure their conjugal domains from every invasion. And in addition, your beloved's face would not be sullied by immodest gazes not her ears by licentious words or her hands by wanton fondling. But she would remain pure and immaculate like an angel's wing and like the ideal maiden, whom St. Basil dreamed of as standing like a modest statue on the pedestal of her maidenhood and "indifferent to all fantasy and contact". The jealous sighs of Tibullus and Byron's invective against women would be incomprehensible to you, like the laments of Jeremiah to one who never had cause to lament. Such then was Joan for Frumentius, a rose without thorns, a fish without bones, a cat without claws; and having lived with men from her childhood, she had none of those eccentricities or even those loveable failings that rendered the daughters of Eve more terrifying even than the Sirens, who were serpents only from the waist down. Seven years had passed since the coming of the young couple to the Monastery of Fulda and Fate continued to spin for them days woven in gold, while their relationship remained secret and untroubled like a pearl in the depths of the sea, nor was their deceit at risk of being discovered for no one prior to the Crusading Frank ever bothered to uncover what lay beneath the complicated words of Plato or the folds of a man's robe. Only the monastery barber would sometimes jest with brother John, when, smiling, the latter would offer his whiskerless cheek, as smooth as a becalmed lake, to the razor.

Yet apart from Joan, there was within the Monastery, unfortunately, another beardless monk; father Corvinus, whom everyone avoided like the inauspicious bird of the same name.[16] When still young, this unfortunate

---

[16] Corvinus from *corvus* in Latin meaning "crow".

Benedictine was in love with the niece of the Bishop of Mainz, whom he served as a deacon, holding the tail of his purple cloak during ceremonies and drinking the water in which His Holiness washed his hands following communion. The young girl had opened first her ears and then her arms to the young deacon's promises of love, but her Episcopal guardian, on coming upon the young couple at night enjoying forbidden fruits in his palace gardens, had his niece's hair shorn; while Corvinus, after being… neutered, was sent to the Monastery at Fulda to repent his sin. At first the young monk had grieved for his loss, just as Jephthah's daughter did for her maidenhood, but time healed the wounds of his body and his soul, and gradually he came to despise women, calling upon his companions to secure Paradise for themselves by making a similar sacrifice, just as the tailless fox in the fable counselled the other foxes to cut their tails off too. This then was the philosophical life that the good Corvinus was leading, making up for the lack of forbidden fruit by tasty meat and the expectation of Paradise, when one day he received an order to get rid of the moths besieging the abbot's library and there he found a translation of St. Basil's discourse *On Virginity*. Opening the book, in which he hoped to discover new reasons to give praise to the Lord for removing from him all means of perdition, he unfortunately fell upon that passage in which the saintly Bishop of Caesaria counsels modest maidens "to guard themselves against male bodies even if they be eunuchs", for just as the bull whose horns have been removed is no less horned by nature and assails those he encounters using that part of his head, where his horns once were, so too the castrated, impassioned by a strange madness, are still able to... But I must refer the reader to the saint's discourse in order to discover the rest of the sentence. According to the critics, Tasso's *Jerusalem* appears to have been written on a shield; St. Basil's discourse appears to me to have been written on the breast of some fair maiden. Reading this passage stirred the monk from his tranquility of so many years. The serpents, dragons, wolves, panthers and other animals, by which the Church Fathers depict passions, were suddenly awakened all together and began to growl and bite their tails in the innermost recesses of his heart, which once again became an ever restless menagerie. Intoxicated with joy, Archimedes shouted "Eureka!" after finding the solution to his problem; the monk, on the other hand, ran around the monastery's cloisters shouting "I'm still able!" in a loud voice. And from that day, he was beset by an unusual obsession, that neither the whip nor dry crusts nor cold baths nor any of the other monastic remedies were able to cure. Totally enthused by the divine eloquence of the Holy Basil, he held the book in his arms night and day, like a new mother her firstborn child, sometimes kissing it and sometimes copying out or learning by heart those sacred pages. Whenever he saw a woman, he ran to her like a thirsty deer to a spring in the wilderness in order to test the words of the Saint. Yet the fair-haired Saxon maids avoided him, albeit that he was castrated, in keeping with the sage counsel of the Bishop of Caesaria, though I consider that even without his counsels, few of these maids knowing his shortcomings would have waited for him to catch up with them.

It was he who was destined to cut the golden thread by which Fate in her kindness had woven together the days of our two lovers, rendering their lives a rosary of shiny and unblemished pearls. Every night Frumentius and Joan went to a cave close to the monastery, which had once been a sanctuary to Priapus. This god was still worshipped in Germany under the name of St. Vitus and his rites had not changed at all. The lips of Christian women continued to ask from him what the impious pagan women had asked, namely pleasures and fertility, and the good saint rarely turned a deaf ear to their pleas. Yet his statues were usually set up in the shade of some male monastery and this, so several slanderous historians say, made certain of the success of the female supplicants. At the back of this sacred cave, behind the wooden statue of the saint, the young couple had made their love-nest, using fragrant leaves of cytisus, fox pelts and soft fabrics of the Orient, votive offerings from the pious ladies of Saxony. Above their bed hung shining stalactites, smoked tongues, dried fish, skeins of fine Moselle wine and other delicacies, to which the young couple had recourse whenever they grew tired of chanting hymns to St. Vitus; for devotion to this saint like that to Aphrodite grows cool without the gifts of Demeter and Bacchus. It was there on some ill-starred night that the two lovers were delighting in all these good things, while their brother Corvinus, unable for some time to enjoy any sleep, which deserts, as parasites do, the unhappy, was roaming like a werewolf in the fields, narrating his torments to the moon. But the moon, tired, it seems, of the monotonous complaining of the poor monk, hid behind some black clouds and before long heavy drops of rain obliged this devotee of St. Basil to seek shelter in the sanctuary of St. Vitus. The fine sand scattered on the floor of the cave to prevent any hurt to the soft feet of the female pilgrims, who could only enter barefoot, concealed the sound of his footsteps so that he proceeded unperceived as far as the hollow where the two lovers were resting in each other's arms and in those of Morpheus. The bed was lit by a lamp burning before the icon of the Christianised Priapus, while Joan was half-naked like an Olympian goddess and so comely was her image as she lay there that even St. Amoun would have forgotten his vows and Origen his woes and also, in my opinion, Themistocles the triumph of Miltiades. As for father Corvinus, he, too, forgetting Frumentius lying beside her, rushed to put to the most rigorous test the physiological theorems of the Bishop of Caesaria. But St. Vitus protected the sleep of the two lovers under his roof; nor was it possible for him to allow his mysteries to be profaned by a vile eunuch. So when he saw Corvinus reaching to put his impudent hand on this sleeping servant, his cheeks flushed with rage, like those of the Madonna of Loreto whenever impious lips kiss her, his head shook menacingly and the oil in the lamp began to boil. A drop of this bubbling oil fell on Frumentius' cheek, awakening him. Leaping to his feet, he saw his beloved still half-asleep and struggling with father Corvinus on top of her as with a bad dream. Frumentius was quick to anger being a veritable descendant of Witikend and of robust build as a German monk, accustomed to using his fists as arguments in every type of discussion, even theological ones. So wasting no time in pointless explanations, he pulled the cord from his waist and began to raise it and bring it down on the back of the wretched Corvinus, like the lash of Jesus on the backs of the moneychangers in the Temple. Meanwhile, Joan got up and hastened to conceal beneath her cassock the cause of the altercation, while the two monks continued to punch each other and the blood to flow, though fortunately only from their noses. After a stubborn fight, Corvinus finally managed to wrestle free from the clutches of his enraged adversary, leaving behind his cowl, like Joseph his garment with the wife of Potiphar. Yet this is where, in my opinion, the similarity ends between him and the son of Jacob.

Remaining alone on the field of battle, the two lovers stared at each other anxiously, certain that the thrashed satyr would betray the secret of their cave, just as Edmond About had revealed everything about Greece in order to exact revenge for his thrashed back. So in order to avoid imprisonment and dry crusts, they would have to bid farewell forever to that hospitable abode, where they had spent such pleasant days in holy respite and idleness, enjoying each other and every bounty. The passing years and soft living had rendered the two monks less adventurous, and with horror they reflected on the travails and deprivations of the wandering life, sharing the opinion of St. Anthony, according to whom monasteries are for monks what the sea is for fish, and just as these die when out of water, so monks too wilt on leaving the coenobia. Such were the gloomy thoughts assailing them when the bell for matins reminded them of the imminent danger. The night was dark and nearby were the stables, in which lived their trusty ass who seven years previously had borne Joan to Fulda. This patriarch of the monastic stalls, already white as snow with age, was resting surrounded by his offspring and by bundles of trefoil. Untying him and muffling his hooves with wads, as pirates do the oars of their boats, the fugitives left behind the walls of that blessed monastery, trembling lest their companion wake the living with his braying just as seven years before he had woken the dead from their graves.

Part III

"But the fact is that I have nothing plann'd
Unless it were to be a moment merry."
                    (Byron, *Don Juan*, Canto IV)

Are you, dear reader, fond of good wine? If you truly are, then of course you hate those unscrupulous innkeepers who, for the sake of profit, adulterate this fine beverage, mixing it with water or colouring or poisonous substances, and instead of divine nectar provide an insipid or nauseous drink for your thirsty lips. Such are the innkeepers who for centuries have supposedly guarded and dispensed the strong wine of faith, as the wise Albinus called religion. The comparison between innkeepers and clerics, between wine casks and Christianity, belongs to some ninth-century Synod, so that my words, if not genteel, are at least "Canonical". I was saying, then, that the true imbiber detests such adulterators of wine, just as the good Christian loathes those who mix religion in order to render it more profitable with whatever their shaven or hairy heads can think of: miraculous icons, pagan

gods disguised as saints, pilgrimages, permits for paradise, sacred relics, rosaries and other hieratic merchandise, by which the missionary's profession is
rendered like to medicine and fortune-telling for its
charlatanism. Being fond of chemistry from childhood, I simply offer in my book a chemical analysis of
religious wine, by which the peoples of the west were
inebriated by cassocked innkeepers during the middle
ages. All harmful animals, serpents, wasps, mosquitoes
and scorpions, become even more venomous and malicious the closer they live to the sun. The one exception are the clerics, who in the sunless lands of the
west acquired sharp claws and poisonous fangs, while
in the east they gradually became harmless and idle
like the eels of Lake Copaïs, for, like them, they are
without taste, yet nor do they bite, like the Franks, but
quietly and honestly go about their work, crossing
themselves, burning incense, baptizing and confessing. Consequently, it would be sinful for anyone to
harm these meek heirs of the Kingdom of Heaven. I
have told you all this, dear reader, to convince you of
my orthodoxy; and now I shall return to my heroes.

Following the death of Charlemagne, there were
neither post houses nor gendarmes nor police any
more in Germany; the Saxon horses were just as today
so big and slow that our two fugitives were not overly
afraid of being pursued. Besides, their mount was one
of those lauded beasts descending from the blessed ass
on which Jesus rode when he entered into Jerusalem,
and on the back of which there remained engraved,

according to the great Albert, the sign of the Cross, just as the image of the divine face remained on Veronica's veil. Such asses, distinguished by a black cross-like streak in the middle of their back, were called "crusaders" and were able, should the need arise, to compete even with horses and dogs in speed and were used in the middle ages only by abbots and prelates. This breed gradually became extinct in Europe but still remains pure and hearty in Egypt and Palestine, where, should you go, dear reader, you will see them bearing gold-trimmed bridles and eating boiled beans from regal pots. It was on such a beast that the fugitives rode in safety like the Red Corsair on his swift ship, with countless plans for their future life together running through their minds. Before long, the sun, rising warm and unclouded behind the peaks of Biberstein, ripened the ideas sprouting in their heads. They decided, then, to travel the world on the ass, seeking hospitality from the powerful, holding out their hands to the lips of the faithful and leaving it to others to take care of the Christianization of the heathens. So they began their wanderings by heading in the direction of Mainz, in order to be present at the ceremony for the reconciliation of the Emperor Louis with his sons. But when, after a three-day journey, they arrived at the city, it was mournful chanting and tolling bells that they heard everywhere in place of joyful songs and, instead of the aroma of roasting meat, it was the fumes of funereal incense that tainted the air. The wretched Louis the *Pious* or the *Debonair* (both adjectives were attributed to him equally as synonyms[1]) had, the previous day, surrendered his blameless soul to his Creator, saying: "I forgive my sons as a condemned man forgives his executioner". His corpse was carried to its final abode by four black horses, which, unfed from the previous day, walked gloomily, like the horses of Hippolytus, between a double line of torch-bearing clerics singing the virtues of the deceased, given that Louis had bequeathed to the Church Sardinia, Corsica and Sicily, which, though occupied by Saracens and Greeks, nominally belonged to him, just as today Cyprus and Jerusalem nominally belong to the Kingdom of Italy.[2] But his good intent was without doubt worthy of praise, incense and litanies. Pulling their cowls down over their faces, our two monks followed the deceased Emperor on that path which, according to Bion, is the easiest of all (given that we all find it even with closed eyes), then in silence they left the walls of grieving Mainz behind them.

Following the death of the pious Louis, the air of Germany was no longer healthy as before for the lungs of those wearing the cassock, many of whom began to migrate, just as the gout-ridden English left Nice following its annexation by France, saying that they had been ordered by their doctor to breathe Italian and not

---

[1] The historians sometimes called him Louis le Pieux and sometimes Louis le Debonnaire.

[2] The Kings of Sardinia, as is well-known, received the title of King of Cyprus and Jerusalem.

Gallic air. Charlemagne's sons took up arms against each other over the paternal inheritance; the elder of these, Lothair, wishing to win over the Saxons to his side, made use, like our own government ministers, of "corrupt means", allowing them to again set up their ancestral idols, and occasionally offer as a sacrificial lamb on the ancestral altars some indiscreet missionary or plump Benedictine. Some slanderous chroniclers even add that this rascally Lothair had idols of Irminsul and Teuton constructed in the palace, which he then sent as conciliatory gifts to the Saxons and Thuringians, just as today the industrialized English send to their colonies statues of Indian or Australian idols, which are manufactured in the factories of London by pious Puritans and Quakers, also loading onto the same ship bundles of bibles from the Bible Society as a form of antidote, so that the idols and Gospels might sail together in peace under the protection of the English flag.

The struggle between Louis' heirs very soon turned Germany into a difficult place to live. The lovers' poor ass stumbled at every step over bodies or slipped in pools of blood and, rarely being able to find barley, grass or leaves, was forced to grind brambles and thistles with its teeth to allay its hunger. What's more, winter was on its way, a Saxon winter, so bitter and harsh that even the crows died of hunger, unable to tear the flesh from the corpses, which were frozen solid by the cold. The poor fugitives wandered like homeless sparrows in the snow, cursing that castrated satyr who had obliged them to leave their warm and cosy nest. The fear of enemies and the harshness of the winter had cooled the hospitality of the Saxons, so that mostly in vain did the two monks knock at the doors of the huts and hamlets. Sometimes they would not even receive any answer, at others a head, blue with cold or pale with fear, would urge the supplicants through a small Saxon door to continue on their way; rarely did a hand, more generous than the head, throw them a crust of black bread or a piece of salted fish for their provisions. In this way, they wandered for two whole months, following like crows in the trail of the armies so as to warm themselves by the embers of a dying fire or to pick the scraps from an abandoned meal. The day came when, enviously gazing at the jackals tearing at the corpses of some of Lothair's soldiers, while hunger tore at their innards like the vulture did at Prometheus' innards, they almost justified the opinion of the wise Chrysippus, who among other things taught his pupils that necrophagia was permissible.

Joan subjected herself to all these hardships without a murmur, enduring the hunger and the cold, as a camel does heat and thirst. Not a sigh or complaint came from her pale lips, with which she sometimes wiped away the tears of her companion, who would often find an occasion to bless the moment in which he had discovered this fair pearl in the current of his life. The character of women can only be compared to Corinthian copper, which is comprised of innumerable heterogeneous elements, but among which, however, there was also pure gold. Thus hungry, tearful, comforting each other, blowing on their fingers and ever journeying south, like swallows and consumptive English ladies, they crossed the snow-covered wastes of the Bavarians, sailed across Lake Constance and finally found hospitality in the Monastery of St. Gallus, where the goodly monks offered them refuge from the wolves and the soldiers of Lothair. The two lovers were already preparing to "cast anchor" under that holy and impregnable roof when a curious monk, looking at Joan carefully, observed that her ears were pierced and, alarmed by this observation, immediately formed strange inklings and desires. All it took was the lobe of a woman's ear to upset the peace of monks in those times, just as today it only takes the smell of a woman's letter to alarm all the inhabitants of Mount Athos. Fearful of any more discoveries and demands on the part of the Holy Father, Joan persuaded Frumentius that they should leave the fold of those inquisitive Swiss the very same day.

From St Gallus they went to Tegernsee, the oldest city in Switzerland, so called because of the strength of its inhabitants and of its schnapps, and from there they arrived at Lucerne, which they entered by night in order better to marvel at the great beacon which, according to the chroniclers, was so bright that it rendered the stars invisible but rendered visible the potholes into which, like the Milesian philosopher, most wayfarers fell. From Lucerne, they made for Aventicum, the capital of the former Ellwangens, where they saw the footprints of Attila outlined in hard rock like those of Jesus were on the Mount of Olives, and from there to Sedunum, where they found a boat in which they sailed down the Rhône as far as Lyon.

This vessel belonged to Jewish merchants on their way to Marseilles to sell Christian slaves to the Spanish Saracens. In those years, these scions of Israel, far from being hounded, were all-powerful in southern France. They loaned large sums to the Emperor on a daily basis and the Emperor paid the interest on his debts by allowing them to proselytise his subjects, just as we tolerate the Sisters of Mercy, the Scripts of the Bible Society, the visions of Agathangelus,[3] the great hopes of similar dreamers and all the fabrications of our three "Protecting" Powers. The Jews of Lyon made use of the Emperor's decrees that they bought as teeth with which to devour the Christians, killing their swine, stealing their children, obliging their slaves to observe the Sabbath and to work on Sundays, selling the recalcitrant like cattle or baptising their children and sometimes even attempting to force the prelates' concubines to convert to Judaism. The poor Bishops sent report after report to the Emperor; while the Jews sent sackful after sackful of money. But while the monarch did not even reply to the former; to the Jews he sent soldiers to guard their houses and to force their debtors to pay what they owed, just as today Christian bailiffs put the

---

[3] Trans. note: Ecumenical Patriarch of Constantinople (1826-1830).

Rothchild's debtors in prison. We are wrong, therefore, to condemn the present century as being more avaricious than previous ones. Gold was always the one God respected throughout the world and the Jews were his prophets. Indeed, in that age, even the Gospels were written in gold letters to render them more venerable.

Among the ship's passengers was an aged rabbi, by the name of Isahar, who, in order to amuse himself during the voyage, attempted to convert the two young monks, seeking, unscrupulous usurer as he was, their souls as payment for the fare. So he began by relating to the young couple that Jesus was a vile Jew, who, having been taught how to work miracles by some enchanter known as John the Baptist, had promised the daughter of the Emperor Tiberius to render her a mother without any male intervention; whereupon, following his advice, the young girl gave birth to a stone instead of a child. Enraged, the Emperor ordered Pilate to crucify the charlatan, whose body was buried close to an aqueduct and was swept away during the night by the floodwaters and this was the source of the Nazarenes' belief concerning his resurrection. After spewing forth all this and more blasphemous prattle, this foulmouthed Jew then began to weave a garland of clouds and stars around the God of Israel. He presented him as sitting, like Bacchus, on a chariot drawn by four panthers: as holding in his right hand a trumpet that was a thousand cubits long and through which he blew his commands into the ears of the Prophets; as giving birth from his head to armed demons, just as

Zeus had given birth to the panoplied Athena; as mixing convivially with the letters of the alphabet, which
were winged angels; and as using huge millstones to
grind the manna from which the bread was made for
the inhabitants of paradise. The two youngsters, sometimes amused by the rabbi's fantasies, sometimes
afraid lest these blasphemies cause the boat to sink
below the waves, muttered by way of an antidote a
hymn to St. Medard, who in those times, like Poseidon
for the ancients and St. Nicholas for us, caused the
waves to swell and to calm.

Thanks to this hymn and the calmness, the boat
moored the next day in Lyon, which at that time was
the seat of St. Agobard, the only saint whose hem even
I would kiss in veneration. He maintained that, since
Jesus is eternal and omnipresent, all those who follow
his commandments whether born before his incarnation or after, whether knowing him or not, were nevertheless Christians and legitimate heirs to the Kingdom
of Heaven. He rejected the worship of holy icons, con-
sidering as disrespectful the representation of an im-
material divinity in the form of a human being, and
teaching that the early Christians kept the images of
Jesus, the Apostles and Martyrs as pictures of people
whom they had known and loved, just as today we
keep photographs of absent friends, and not as objects
of superstitious worship. Apart from these things,
the goodly Bishop also considered it foolish for us to
believe that the Almighty dictated the Scriptures to the
prophets word by word as the angel did the maxims to

Barlaam's ass. He discouraged the faithful from undertaking pilgrimages, ordered that their alms be given
to the poor and not to the Church, regarding it as a
sin, when there were so many paupers without even a
copper to buy bread, that gold should be given to the
clergy to light candles in broad daylight or to decorate
the statues in their churches,[4] or the breasts of their
concubines. Such were the Christian or rather eternal
truths taught by this goodly servant of the Almighty,
which if he had proclaimed any later, would have seen
him burned like Hus or cast unwept and unburied
onto the rocks like Caires.[5] Yet in those times, the
priests in the west, concerned as they were exclusively
with debauchery and charlatanism, had not yet become obsessed by the mania to condemn and burn
human beings. If in the midst of that general ignorance and corruption, someone should have the peculiar wish to live virtuously or speak rationally, the
others would devour this good man's share, laughing
at his foolishness and leaving for him the title of saint,
which was then bestowed freely on priests just as today
the title of "eminence" is on the doctors. Such then was
Agobard, a diamond among pebbles, a swan among

---

[4] In the western churches, apart from the icons, there were also
statues of the Virgin, clad in silken robes and adorned with ear-
rings and necklaces.

[5] Trans. note: Theophilus Caires (1784-1852), whose writings
caused him to be excommunicated. After death, his body was
refused Christian burial.

crows, shining in the darkness of the ninth century as a pearl in a swine's snout.[6] Encountering him, while with great toil and disgust I was raking through all the dung of the middle-ages, I wished to repose for a few moments beside him, like the weary Arab beside a desert oasis. To such a man one is reluctant to give the ridiculous and ignominious title of saint, just as among us every honourable person is ashamed to wear the cross of the Saviour.

Frumentius went together with Joan to kiss the hands of the good Bishop. The travellers of those times, on arriving in a strange city, would seek the residence of the Prelate just as today they seek the Consulate. There they submitted their letters of introduction and sought guidance and help that they might continue their journey, in exchange for which they usually presented the Bishop with some holy relic from their birthplace; given that it was common among the Christians then to collect holy relics from every land and era, like recently Athenians have taken to stamp-collecting. So our travellers, having much to ask for but nothing to offer His Holiness, presented themselves before him, shy and reserved, just as the hungry widows of our revolutionary heroes present themselves on the doorstep of the political toadies. But St. Agobard, accustomed like the confessors and doctors to "examining kidneys and hearts", knew how to dis-

---

[6] Proverbs 11, 22.

cern the worth hidden beneath the rags. Inviting that much afflicted couple into his frugal dining room, he marvelled at the beauty of his young guests, their wisdom and brotherly love, comparing them to Castor and Pollux and, when they left, he gave them good advice, new footwear, his blessing and money for the rest of their journey.

So after six days of again sailing down the Rhône, the travellers reached Arles, the then famous base of Constantine the Great, now renowned for its figs and maidens who, like the English horses, owe their beauty to intermingling with the Arabs. After marvelling at the remains of the imperial residence, the cathedral, the amphitheatre and the obelisk, the two wayfarers felt the need to take care for their stomachs, which had been empty for some time like the temple of Athena, before which they found themselves at that moment. Whereupon, they made for the local nunnery, the oldest in the whole of France, which had been founded by St. Caesarius in the sixth century and who wrote, so it is said, the rules in his own blood, as Dracon did his laws and Henry III his letters to his mistress.[7] These rules were severe and harsh like the cassock of their saintly redactor. No stranger, either man or woman, was allowed to enter the nunnery; as for the nuns, they were not permitted even to show their heads through the door. Those who bathed their bodies, combed their

---

[7] See Chateaubriand, *Analyse raisonnée de l'histoire de la France.*

hair, revealed their teeth when smiling or their feet when walking were flogged or thrown in chains into the dungeons. But these voluptuous daughters of warm Provence were unable to submit themselves for very long to such laws. The poor maidens waned in the nunnery like plants in a botanist's pot until, trampling upon their aged abbess and the monstrous rules of St. Caesarius, they acquired their freedom and together their colour and vivacity. Since then, they have organized themselves constitutionally, have constructed a theatre in the nunnery, are allowed to go out twice a week and fast whenever they have toothache. When the pious Louis attempted to bring these straying lambs back under the yoke of St. Benedict, they replied in a plenary council that they owed obedience only to their abbess, that they would observe fasting and chastity as much as possible, but neither by vow nor promise were they willing to be bound, afraid, so they said, lest they "add to the sins of the flesh that of perjury too". This was the situation then in most of the "nunneries" in Europe, which were referred to as "sinneries" by St. Peter Damian.

As happens often in Provence, the sun, forgetting that it was still winter, was high in the sky and warming the slabs of the nunnery courtyard when the two travellers presented themselves at the entrance. The gatekeeper was snoring beside the open gate; the travellers passed by her and roamed for a while through empty cloisters and silent corridors before finally coming to the dormitory where, in keeping with the custom in warm climes, the nuns were taking their siesta. Wicker screens protected the eyes of the sleeping maidens from the midday sun, while the dim light rendered even more comely these habit-clad Aphrodites. Among these brides of Jesus, just as in the Sultan's harem, could be found maidens of every race and colour: redheads from Switzerland, as white as the milk of their goats and as placid as their country's lakes, and newly-converted Saracens, black as coal and as hot, smiling Galatians and mountain-born Pyrenean shepherdesses. The dormitory resembled those botanical gardens in which are found flowers of all kinds differing in colour, fragrance and origin, yet similar in beauty, all blossoming in captivity within their glass prison. Some of the sleeping nuns, given over to voluptuous dreams, were smiling and supporting their burning cheek on their arms, while their heaving breasts appeared beneath their white camisole like the moon behind the clouds. Some, pale and sullen, resembled a statue of sleeping Sorrow, perhaps seeing in their dreams the shores of their homeland or their mother's lips. Others appeared as if holding out a hand to the Abbess' rod and others as if opening their arms to their heavenly suitor. But most of them were sleeping quietly and peacefully like the Pharaoh in the Great Pyramid; some were in fact snoring but these were the old ones dreaming of the bliss of paradise.

The two lovers had forgotten their hunger while marvelling at those diverse personifications of Morpheus when suddenly the cry was heard of the silver

cock which adorned the dormitory clock, a masterpiece of Arabian art, donated by a Saracen ruler who
had been shown hospitality in the nunnery where he
found, according to some wicked tongues, all the pleasures of his palace. At this sound, a multitude of eyes,
black, blue, grey and brown, opening from their slumber, twinkled like stars in the dimness of the room and
fixed themselves with curiosity on the two unexpected
strangers. Nuns in those times were neither prudish
nor timid and there was nothing frightening in the appearance of our two heroes; on the contrary, brother
Frumentius was ruddy and staunch like a Dutch tulip,
while Joan was graceful and fresh like a meadow vio-
let. These monastic maidens, loving flowers as do all
prisoners, rushed up to the young monks with a noisy
flurry of white like waves of the sea, asking who they
were and how they had come to be in their dormitory.
After they had satisfied their curiosity, they took care
to satisfy the strangers' hunger, inviting them to join
them at the supper table, where for the first time these
children of the freezing north tasted the sweet fruits of
the south, the figs and raisins, about which the erudite
Joan asked, licking her lips and fingers, whether they
were the sweet lotus fruit.

The two lovers rested for three months with the
hospitable maidens, who were permitted by the rules
to have with them confessors and gardeners in order
to "subdue their souls and water the nunnery gardens",
as the goodly Chroniclers used to say, who naturally
couldn't imagine how much misunderstanding and

vile puns they were creating for the enemies of religion by this phrase, which is no more than a squiggle for my innocent pen. At first, things could not have gone better; both of them gained weight and quite forgot their homeland beneath the clear sky of Provence, beneath which today the natives of Chios have forgotten their fragrant isle. "Where one is well, there is the homeland," said Euripides. The honeyed fruit of the lotus grows everywhere and offers itself in all kinds of forms to the insatiable lips of mortals, like thrones to kings and a comely maiden to lovers, like gold to merchants and like applause to artists. And even in snowy mountain peaks and desert sands, the lotus once blossomed when the hermits sought sainthood there and slaves their freedom, but today it has become a garden plant like the leek and perhaps for this reason the poets have banished it from Mount Helicon.

We were saying then that the two monks, once again finding their ease, were gaining weight and living happily in the female fold. But before long Joan succumbed to an unknown and terrible illness. Her cheeks became hollow like the ships of the Achaeans; her eyes dim and lacklustre like stars in the morning. Instead of food she chewed her nails and instead of sleeping she sighed all night long. Her companion kept asking her what was wrong, but she replied only with tears and moans and whenever he went to kiss her, she turned her back to him rather than her cheek, sometimes sending him to kiss sister Martha and sometimes the holy Bathilde or one of the other maidens. The goodly Frumentius, accustomed to obeying his sweetheart's every command, rushed to carry out her requests, but when he returned to seek his reward for his willing obedience, the poor young man received curses instead of thanks and fingernails instead of lips.

Having described the symptoms, I consider it unnecessary to name the ailment. My poor young heroine's position was ever more pitiful given that, though burning with constant jealousy, she was unable even to repay her lover with the same coin, but was devoid of weapons beneath that male attire like a tiger in a metal cage. The nuns heaped conjecture upon conjecture like the giants mountain upon mountain, trying to divine what manner of madness it was that had beset this fair and comely young monk, who not only rejected their tenderness like rabid dogs do water, but also became enraged at his companion whenever he saw him conversing with them. At the turn of this century, all ailments were attributed to inflammation of the stomach and under the name of gastritis were treated without exception by the bloodthirsty Broussais using leeches. In the ninth century, however, all the mental and physical illnesses were attributed to possession by demons, so that the only cure was exorcism and the use of saintly relics. Theology and medicine, from which we expect the salvation of our soul and body, are the only disciplines that are subject, like clothes, to fashion. All that our ancestors believed we today call mythology, while the barbershop doctors mock the prescriptions of Galen and Paracelsus.

Heaven only knows what our descendents will say, reading the papers on Chromhidrosis[8] by the Paris medical academy or Pope Pius' decree concerning the immaculate conception by St. Anne, or of the wonders of pepsin and the miraculous icon of Tinos.

Following a meeting of the nunnery council, it was decided to send brother John for healing to St. Bona, to the Holy Grotto of St. Magdalen, where a tree had grown, the fragrance of which drove out demons and cured the blind like the smoke from fish during the time of Tobias.[9] So, helping his demonized sweetheart up onto the faithful ass, the goodly Frumentius despondently made for the Holy Grotto, ofttimes turning his head to look back and cursing both eunuchs and demons, who were constantly driving him to new shores like the curse of Jesus did the Jewish sandal-maker.

Jealousy, when it is not an idiopathic or "constitutional"[10] ailment, like sinecurism in Greece, is always a

---

[8] An illness that was unknown prior to 1862, characterized by black sweat flowing from the eyelids and stemming from the adulteration of the liquids or, according to others, from some black dye placed by the patients upon their eyebrows. See the various articles on this in the *Gazette des Hopitaux* of the aforementioned year.

[9] "If someone is bothered by a demon, the heart and liver (of the fish) should be smoked before the man or woman and they will never be bothered again, while the bile may be used to cure someone who has a glaucoma." Tobias 6, 7-8.

[10] *Syphil… Constitutionelle* as it appears on the wrapping paper of antisyphil… tablets sold in Constantinople.

severe and annoying illness, but the good thing is that it goes away immediately once the underlying causes are removed, like seasickness when the ship reaches port. In this way our heroine also ceased to be tormented by the wicked demon once the presence of her rivals ceased to sharpen his claws and fangs. Before they had reached even half-way, Joan had already regained her appetite and her good spirits so that there remained little for the saint to do in order to bring about a complete cure. Arriving after a journey of three days at the foothills of the mountain, on the summit of which was the grotto, the two monks began with difficulty to climb the steep slopes, followed by their ass who, plodding along without food from the previous day, shook its head gloomily as though it were tired of its miserable life. The first parents of this wretched beast perhaps also ate some stalks of forbidden barley in some corner of paradise so that their descendents are still paying as we are for their original sin. After climbing for two hours, the three pilgrims finally set foot on a wooded plateau, in the centre of which was the entrance to the dark grotto, where for thirty years the fair daughter of Gennesaret had wept for her sins. In the middle of this grotto was a hollow carved into the rock by the saint's tears, which on falling were transformed into pearls that were distributed to the poor by the saint. Next to this hollow rested the saint's corpse, placed there by Saints Lazarus, Trophimus and Maximinus on coming to France, where in those times the persecuted disciples of Jesus sought refuge like today the followers of Mazzini go to Great Britain. A fragrant and evergreen sapling shaded the tomb, indicating to the pilgrims where they should fall to their knees. So bending their knees before it, the lovers began with a humble voice and heart to chant the hymn of this sanctified concubine, whose sins rendered more women sinners than her repentance did saints. We all aspire to resemble somewhat great men, imitating their failings, whenever we are unable to imitate their virtues. Many became drunkards in order to have something in common with Alexander the Great, while the courtiers of Louis removed their teeth in order to resemble their monarch. But the transgressions of the fair Magdalen and her saintliness attracted infinitely more imitators. It is she who the few good remaining Christian women have as their model and idol, biting the forbidden fruit, while they still have teeth, and then offering their wrinkles and their wigs to God as the price for entering paradise.

While our two pilgrims were calling upon the grace of the saint, the ass, which had followed them into the grotto, seeking refuge from the sun, sniffed the sapling shading the saint's tomb with increasing appetite. For a long time the poor beast had not tasted fresh food, but having received a monastery upbringing had learned to respect what was holy and thus in its heart an intense struggle was taking place between hunger and piety. Its eyes glazed, its nostrils flared, it kept opening and closing its mouth, slightly licking those fragrant leaves with the tip of its tongue like a lover does the hands of his sleeping beloved, afraid lest he wake her. Yet it was hunger that prevailed over every other sensation and closing its long ears as its kind are wont to do whenever they are getting ready to do some foolishness, it shook that wondrous sapling so vehemently with its teeth that it remained uprooted in its profane mouth. On seeing the altar before which they were praying being snatched away, the two lovers leapt up in horror, fixing their terrified gaze on the sacrilegious beast and an even more terrified gaze at the profuse blood dripping from the roots of the plant, while from the open hole could be heard heart-rending cries like those of Polydorus when Aeneas pulled out the arrows planted in his body, and amidst these cries sounded a mournful woman's voice cursing the greedy animal: "this blood flows from my heart and not from that insentient stem. A curse on you for rending it. May you sag beneath a heavy load and be beaten every day of your life!" From that day forth, asses, like Jews, are subject to this double curse. Both, scattered over the face of the earth, cursed, beaten and despised, pay not only for the original sin that afflicts us all, but also the price of a second sin; the ones the sin of deicide, the others the sin of sacrilegious greed. As for the ass responsible for this second downfall, it was even more unfortunate than Adam: not being able even to digest the forbidden fruit, but succumbing to terrible spasms, it straightaway surrendered its spirit like Ozas before the ark of the Almighty. Thenceforth, Provence's blind, lame, possessed and paralysed and all who previously had been cured by Magdalene's tree, came every year to the place where the unburied bones of the remover of their miraculous cure lay, and there they heaped a plethora of curses on its memory and a plethora of wounds on the backs of its descendents.

The two pilgrims, whose hairs were standing on end in horror and whose teeth were rattling like the castanets of a Spanish dancer, sped back down the mountain like an avalanche in the Pyrenees, not stopping till they saw in the distance the azure waters of the Mediterranean. Then resting for a few hours in the shade of a beech, they once again walked all night long, arriving the next morning at Toulon with their ears still ringing with the ass-killing curses of Magdalene and the death rattle of the wretched beast.

The harbour of Toulon was deserted save for a single Venetian trireme, which, having transported from Alexandria to Venice the body and the handwritten gospel of St. Mark, was sailing along the coasts of Provence to purchase slaves with a view to exchanging them in the ports of the Orient for incense, cotton and holy relics. Those years were the golden age of slavery. Venetians, Amalfians, Pisans and Genoese roamed around like Mediterranean sharks, rivalling each other as to who could buy more human beings from the bandit chieftains and brigands who, after the death of Charlemagne, ravaged Galatia and Italy, plying their trade freely and untroubled, just as they do today in Attica. But these at least, instead of robbing the relatives too by seeking a ransom, lit fires on the seashore in order to inform the buyers on their ships, to whom they sold the captive that very same day, thus benefitting rather than causing loss to his heirs. And though the clergy anathematized those plying this trade, nevertheless they also accepted from them gold-embroidered robes, costly perfumes, gem-studded crosses and other products of their work, just as today the English black-sympathisers inveigh against the slave trade while adding to their tea sugar and rum, the sweat and blood of the blacks. Indeed some poisonous tongues put it about that many of the officials at the papal court, including the Master of Ceremonies, were secretly in league with the brigand leaders with the aim to enrich and embellish the Church.

The ship was ready to set sail and a rowing boat was waiting on the shore for the return of the captain, who had gone to meet his Jewish agent in order to complete the cargo. Presently, this honest seadog followed by eight seamen, holding a whip in their right hand and in their left a rope, at the end of which were tied, two by two like partridges in the marketplace, the newly-bought slaves, sixteen in number, nine humans and seven women; and I say humans and not men because in those times it was still doubted whether women in fact belonged to the human race. Those who denied women their humanness pointed to their affairs with goats in Egypt and with horses in Thessaly, the opinion of Aristotle, their wickedness, the daughter of Aristoxenus, who had the legs of an ass, and the

— 138 —

verse by Tobias.[11] The captain was a Ragusan, a fisher-
man and pagan in his youth who, when initiated into
the mystery of faith, wished to imitate the Apostle by
becoming himself a "fisher of men", whom he hooked
and sold just as previously he had done with fish. Seeing the two lovers who, huddling inside their robes,
were sitting dejectedly like castaways on the steps of
the quayside, he thought that it would be good to take
these two followers of St. Benedict on board in order to
help the hangman maintain good order among the
captives, threatening the discontented with the fires of
Hell as he with the noose. This experienced seaman
was at the same time deeply knowledgeable concerning
politics, realizing like the then kings that only through
the clerics and hangmen could people be rendered a
docile herd ready to offer their backs to the shears. The
poor young couple, having tasted so much of the bitter-
ness that arises on dry land, readily accepted the slave-
dealer's proposal, hoping to finally find rest on the
waves like Noah in the ark, access to which was denied
to anything evil with the exception of tigers, serpents,
scorpions and the lice that were to be found in the Patriarch's beard. So the oars sliced the waves and, before
long, sailors, slaves, captains and monks set foot on the
deck of the *St. Porcarius* as this godly ship was named.

The two lovers seated themselves on a pile of rope
in the prow, gazing at the coast of verdant Provence

---

[11] See the reference above, p. 133.

receding in the distance. Jealousy had rekindled Joan's love, while her caprices had done the same for Frumentius, so that they huddled up to each other enjoying the delights of reconciliation and making countless plans concerning their future life together. The ship was sailing to Alexandria but they intended to disembark in Athens and there, between the columns of the Parthenon and the laurel trees of the Illyssos, to make their nest. Joan's stepfather, being descended from Greeks, as we said, had taught his wife's daughter the language and history of his ancestors so that our heroine's tiny feet danced for joy at the prospect of standing before long on the land that covered the ashes of Pericles and Aspasia, while her supposedly Greek blood bubbled in her veins like the waters of the Jordan when the body of the Saviour submerged itself in them. Meanwhile, the ship was already sailing by the fragrant coasts of Santa Margherita. The day was warm; the sun was shining behind milky clouds like the face of a young Turkish girl behind the folds of her yashmak; the sea was slumbering like a bishop after a meal and there were white cranes, too, travelling in the sky. There is nothing more pleasant, in such weather, than to be on the deck of a "swift-winged ship" waiting after breakfast for suppertime with one's head on the beloved's lap and marvelling together with her at the beauty of the sky, the earth and the water. Both the stomach and the heart need to be satisfied in order that we may be able to marvel at nature; otherwise the sun seems to us, to me at least, a machine for ripening melons, the moon a lantern for robbers, the trees firewood, the sea saltwater and life tasteless like an overboiled pumpkin.

After a three-day voyage, the ship put in at the harbour of Aleria, capital of Corsica, where the crew went ashore to get water and the two monks went ashore too to venerate all the island's holy relics that were renowned throughout the world, because kept there was the rod of Moses, some balls of clay from which Adam had been fashioned, a rib of the Apostle Barnabas, a phial containing drops of the Madonna's milk, a piece of cloth woven by her sacred hands and other ancient things no less sacred or original, which even today the pious pilgrim can venerate. The next day, with the help of a strong wind, they passed Sardinia, famous according to the poets for its cheeses and for the treachery of its inhabitants; while on the third day the wind abated... But being only a mediocre swimmer, I am unable to follow the course of the ship bearing my heroine as I did the tracks of her deceased ass. Besides, nautical descriptions, waves, ropes, tar and shipwrecks are all as well-worn as a postman's shoes and provoke only nausea in the reader like the rolling of a ship on the sea, unless, that is, some amusing episode of hunger or cannibalism is inserted. So referring those with a thirst for such punishment to Mr P. Soutsos' sugary descriptions, in which not the slightest poetic air comes to disturb the

quiet shore, all smiling sweet,

we would like to inform the other readers that the
waves caused our heroes to yawn, to vomit, to sleep
and to suffer all the other things that befall passengers
before they eventually, after a two-month voyage,
arrived safely at Corinth and, disembarking there,
journeyed by way of Megara to Athens, guided by a
young Greek slave named Theonas who was a present
to them from the captain.

The sun, bright and cloudless like the sun that
ripened the apples of Eden, was rising behind Hymettus when the three travellers, skirting the Poikile Stoa,
entered the city of Hadrian. Crowds of Athenians
were gathering from all directions in the churches in
order to celebrate the Sunday of Orthodoxy, namely
the restoration of the holy icons. Swept along by
them, the three travellers entered the Theseion, which
was then a Christian church dedicated to St. George.
Christianity crushed idolatry and yet this innocent
victim rendered its murderer its main heir, bequeath-
ing to it its temples, rites, sacrifices, seers, priests and
soothsayers. Appropriating all these things, the Christians put them to their own use as plagiarists do others' ideas, calling the temples churches, the sacrificial
tables altars, the processions litanies and the gods
saints: Poseidon became St. Nicholas, Pan became St.
Demetrius and Apollo the Prophet Elijah. In addition,
the clerics gave them long beards to render them
more venerable, like the procurers of Rome gave
blonde wigs to their wards to attract more clients. But
let us get back to Athens.

Following the death of the profane Theophilus, who cut off the hands of the painters and smeared the holy icons with whitewash as nursemaids do their breasts with aloe that the suckling infants may find them repulsive, the poor eastern Christians, already being deprived of their icons for eleven years, doubly felt their longing because of this long deprivation. So the "orthodox" monks and painters outlawed by the tyrant came down from the mountains; in fact, according to some hagiographers, not only did the living swarm into the churches, but many of the dead martyrs rose from their graves, too, in order to take part in that joyous rite, during which the icons spoke and the coals jumped with joy in the censers. Yet even than the most belligerent iconoclasts were suddenly transformed into fervent icon-worshippers when the god-unbeloved Theophilus was succeeded by the god-given Theodora.[12] Parents stuck their children's hair onto the icons, monks offered their hair to them as a sacrifice, while the women removed their pigments, like their ancestors did the phallus of Priapus, and like them mixed the pigments with water and drank them; even the priests would often attempt, using these pigments, to adulterate the sacred communion wine. In Athens, that classical seat of idols, the zeal of the faithful became such that the Bishop was obliged to cover the icons with glass in order that,

---

[12] Trans. note: in Greek, a pun on the literal meaning of the two names, i.e. "beloved of God" and "gift of God".

kissed by so many lips, they would not, after a few days, become pale and faded like the image of the Saviour on Veronica's kerchief. According to the lawyers, every new transgression of the law gives rise to a new law; so too in the Church of Christ, each new heresy creates the orthodox dogma. The excesses of iconoclasm gave rise to iconolatry, the Son became "Consubstantial" with the father despite the Arians; the Virgin was named Mother of God to refute the blasphemies of Nestorius; and Pope Pius IX, in order to punish the impious doubts of his faithless subjects concerning her immaculate conception, imposed on them as an article of faith the immaculate pregnancy by her mother Anna in addition. Who knows what new things may sprout from the blasphemous book by Renan, which, according to His Holiness the Abbé Crelier, "has already greatly benefitted religion," providing both him and his followers with the means to prove "the Truth to be clear" like the light of the sun.

On entering the Theseion with their servant, the two lovers were barely able to find a narrow corner for themselves in the packed church. That morning, the mass was being said by the Bishop of Athens, Nicetas, who was as shiny as a new florin in his gold vestments. These two children of the North marvelled at the luxuriance of this servant of God, who taught poverty, promising the faithful in exchange for this a paradise strewn with gold, sapphires, emeralds and amethysts after death. But the clergy of the time preferred the egg today rather than the chicken tomorrow, leaving to those successors of the Cynics, the ascetics, the torn robes, the lice and the emeralds of Paradise, while they, in all their gold finery, officiated in those same temples where, according to Plutarch, no pagan ever dared to enter wearing gold. Meanwhile, Theonis, who had experience as a verger, leaned over to Joan's ear to explain to her the rites of our mass; for example, how the Eastern Christians make the sign of the cross using three fingers to symbolize the Holy Trinity, putting these first to the forehead in memory of the Father in Heaven, then to the belly, symbolizing Jesus' descent into Hades, then to the right shoulder, because the Son sits at the right hand of the father, and finally to the left to drive Satan from their hearts. Then he explained to her the name and the use of each of the sacred vestments of the officiating prelate, of the girdle, which "girdled him with power", of the knee-piece, which is as a sword by his thighs,[13] of the cope, the triangles of which symbolize Jesus Christ, the cornerstone of the Church, and of the spear, which the priest used to pierce the offertory bread in memory of the spear plunged by the Roman soldier into the side of the Saviour. While Theonis was recounting all this, the officiating priest cut a second loaf of bread, transforming it into the body of the Virgin, whose actual presence in the sacrament was at that time believed by the Eastern Christians, since one day, while the priest was

---

[13] Psalms 44, 4.

chanting the "Hail Mary", the offertory bread was suddenly transformed into the Virgin, who was visible with her Son in her arms. The remaining loaves were blessed in the name of St. John the Baptist, the prophets, the martyrs and the other saints. After these, mention was also made of the living, namely of the Archbishop, the priests, the Church benefactors and others. Once they had all received their allotted share of the victim as in the past, in that same temple during the feast of Theseus, the deacon incensed the holy altar and the asterisk,[14] following which he chanted the "de profundis" and then… Yet I consider that there is no need for us, dear reader, to follow the service to the end, which in any case was Byzantine just as it is today and, according to the Catholics, will remain like that throughout the centuries as punishment for the schism, impervious to the rise of civilisation and attached to the ceremonies of the middle ages like a limpet to the rock.

The two Germans marvelled at the length of that endless service, which was an abridgement of the abridgement of the collection of St. James, yet the descendents of Pericles also stared in wonder at those two foreigners like a naturalist might at some strange product of the animal kingdom, unable as they were to reconcile their cassocks with their beardless faces and

---

[14] Trans. note: an ornament used in the Orthodox liturgy to cover the chalice.

short hair. When the mass ended and everyone had received the communion offering, a circle of curious heads formed around these two children of the west who were examined from head to toe and plied with questions as to whence they had come and why, as monks, they were not ashamed to shave their beards and, even more repugnant, to wear undergarments, which was considered by the eastern monks to be an unforgivable indulgence. Joan and Theonas were barely able to respond to all these questions, while the human chain tightening around them made it difficult for them even to breathe. Frumentius, who knew neither Greek nor had very much patience, was already endeavouring to open a way through with his fists when, by good fortune, the bishop arrived to free them, reproaching his flock for their indiscretion. Then taking the two strangers into his pontifical palanquin, carried by eight newly-converted Bulgarians who served His Eminence as horses, he brought them to the Episcopal palace on the slopes of the Acropolis, where a great banquet had been prepared to celebrate the restoration of the icons.

The table was laid outside in the garden in the leafy shade of an old plane tree and was sagging under the weight of dishes and viands, the aromas of which mixed with the fragrant smells of the plants. Before very long, the guests began to arrive. Most of these were Orthodox monks who had taken refuge in caves and in the hills during the time of the Iconomachy so as not to be forced by Theophilus to spit on the holy icons or to marry a nun in the midst of the market-place. These goodly hermits had become fierce and frightening in appearance as a result of their long co-habitation with the beasts of the wild. They included Father Bathaeus, whose mouth was crawling with worms from excessive fasting; Athanasius, who never washed his face or feet or ate cooked food because whenever he saw the temporary fire of the kitchen he was reminded of the everlasting fire of Hell and wept; Meletius, whose body was covered from head to toe in putrid ulcers like Job. But, in order to find relief, Job scratched himself with a potsherd, whereas whenever a worm fell to the ground from his wounds, the blessed Meletius would pick it up and put it back in its place in order to have greater pain in his body and a corresponding reward for his soul.

Together with these came Father Paphnutius, who was ever immersed in heavenly ecstasy and little con-cerned with worldly things with the result that, when thirsty, it often happened that, instead of water, he would drink the oil from his lamp; blessed Tryphon, who never wore a clean shirt, but preferred the un-washed clothes of his superior; the hermit Nicon who, having succumbed to the sins of the flesh, repented by shutting himself in a graveyard, where he remained for thirty years, sleeping on his feet like horses do and eating only the greens which sprouted from the earth watered by his tears. These were followed by other monks from the hills who carried staffs to support their slow and shaky steps. Some of these were missing

limbs like ancient Greek statues and all without exception were filthy, lice-ridden and had the unbearable
stench of fasting, sainthood and garlic. Poor Joan
recoiled in horror before those repugnant products of
eastern fanaticism, sometimes holding her nose,
sometimes closing her eyes, unsure as to whether they
were human beings and involuntarily recalling all she
had learned from the ancients concerning dog-headed
and apelike men or read in the legendaries concerning
the Satyrs who lived together with St. Anthony in the
deserts of Thebes and discoursed with him on theological matters. But these foul-smelling and maggot-
eaten skeletons, for whom pleasure and loss, hell and
cleanliness were synonymous words, these monks,
recluses, hermits and ascetics that I am referring to,
the very memory of whom today gives rise to pity and
disgust, were held in great esteem during the reign of
the pious Theodora, as the charioteers were under
Michael III, the apes under Pope Julius and the students in the district of Hafteia in the days of our own
interim reign. Consequently, the ambitious and ingra-
tiating Bishop Nicetas was obliged to take good care of
them just as our parliamentary candidates have to
shake hands with the scoundrels in the marketplace
and the brigands in the hills. Also invited to the
Bishop's table, in addition to these monks, were two
teachers of Greek letters, an astrologer and three
eunuchs from the Byzantine Court, who had come to
Athens with the Imperial Decree concerning the resti-
tution of the icons.

Once they had all taken their places and recited "For what we are about to receive…", Nicetas broke a piece of bread and offered it on a silver dish to the icon of the Virgin, who during the banquets of the Christians of the time always received the first portion like the daughter of Rhea[15] did with the ancients. Then the Bishop took care of his guests, digging his knife into the belly of a fatted kid, from which immediately emanated a delicious aroma of garlic, onion and leek, with which the animal had been stuffed with great dexterity. After the kid, fish seasoned with caviar was served and then mutton with honey and quince. Accustomed to the simple and unseasoned food in Germany in those times, where even the banquets began and ended as in the *Iliad* with roasted meat, Joan stuck her fork hesitantly and disbelievingly into those intricate products of Byzantine cuisine, like the European travellers do with the suspicious stews of the Athenian hotels. When, next, she tasted the Attic wine blended with pitch, gypsum, and resin, she turned her mouth away in disgust, afraid lest the Athenians were offering her hemlock to drink like Socrates or vinegar mixed with gall like the Jews gave to Jesus. As an alternative, though this caused our German girl even more disgust, the monk beside her offered her another glass filled with some monkish tonic called *Acornio*, probably discovered by St. Anthony by boiling his swine's

---

[15] Hestia.

acorn feed, and which can be found even today in Greek schools, where it is given to the poor pupils instead of coffee. Consequently, Joan and Frumentius sat at that well-laid table hungry and thirsty, like the French emissaries at the banquets of Nicephorus, till the hospitable Nicetus pitied them and ordered roast turtle-doves to be served, together with honey from Mt. Hymettus and pure wine from Chios. At the sight of the red jug containing that divine wine, the gloomy faces of the good ascetics lit up with joy, like Hades when Jesus descended there, and all of them willingly held out their glass to the crimson nectar from Homer's birthplace, thus proving that human nature is subject, like pregnant women, to peculiar appetites, capable of liking *Acornio*, filth, swine and retsina, but when something pure and good appears in any form, human nature immediately turns to it like a magnet to the north pole and like Nicetas' guests to the jug from Chios. In my view, it is sophistry to say that every people or every person has their own idea of what is good; the proverb *De gustibus non est disputandum* is incorrect. Moulded from the same dough were the eyes, ears and lips of all of Adam's descendants; *For we being many are one bread, and one body*[16] and everyone likes Circasian maidens, Indian diamonds, Arabian horses, the columns of the Parthenon, the grapes of Constantinople, the legs of Spanish women, ice in the mid-

---

[16] 1 Corinthians 10, 17.

dle of summer, Italian cantatas and French wines; while even the blacks of Africa prefer white women rather than Ethiopians. If in one of our own churches, there were to appear one of Raphael's Madonnas or, suddenly, there were to be heard one of the sacred melodies of Rossini or Mozart, it would be to these, I think, that the truly orthodox eyes and ears would turn, while truly deserving of the name of Schismatics would be those who preferred the gloomy Byzantine icons and nasal droning.

Nicetas kept pouring out the wine for his guests, quoting the verse from Proverbs, "and drink of the wine which I have mingled"[17] and the monks kept holding out their glasses, chanting the verse from Isaiah "Come ye, say they, I will fetch wine and we will fill ourselves with strong drink...",[18] but before they drank, they piously closed their eyes in keeping with the express command of Solomon forbidding wine-drinkers to look at the wine before drinking it,[19] just as Mohammed forbade the Turks to look at their wives before marrying them. If one gets drunk easily, it means that he is not a drunkard, just as desiring every woman one sees denotes continence. Thus the

---

[17] Proverbs 9, 5.

[18] Isaiah 56, 12.

[19] *Non intuearis vinum quandum flavescit* (Proverbs 1, 4), though, according to the Septuagint, the verse is as follows: "If you lend your eye to the glass and the bottle, later you will walk more naked...".

heads of these goodly ascetics, who for so many years had known only prayer and the intoxication of heavenly ecstasy, began before very long to spin like the earth around the sun. Yet though drunk, these holy hermits spoke only of saintly matters. As old soldiers take pleasure in recounting, after dinner, their battles and their victories, so the hermits too began to expound on their miracles and their exploits. One recounted how, having been treated to a few beans by some poor man who had nothing else to give, he planted in his beard a grain of wheat, which soon multiplied, so that this goodly fellow, shaking his beard, was able to fill fifty sacks of wheat. Another recounted how, on the order of the abbot, he had planted in the monastery garden his pastoral staff, which, watered every day for three years with his tears, blossomed and produced many and varied fruits: apples, apricots, figs and grapes, so that all his brothers ate their fill. Blessed Nicon recounted how, longing in his heart to see the renowned beauty of the Virgin, he had fasted and prayed night and day till, taking pity on him, the merciful Madonna had appeared before him in such beauty and radiance that he was blinded in one eye and would have been totally blinded had he not managed to close one eye. Afterwards, it was the turn of Blessed Pangratius, whose staff made the rocks sprout lilies, then of the Athenian hermit Aegidius, whose shadow cured the sick that it passed over, so that whenever he was walking through the city streets, the ailing jostled with each other over it just as the ancients did over an ass's shadow. Then there was Bathaeus, who was cooled by the flames instead of burned, like the Dutch by pepper. These and other "marvels" were recounted by the goodly ascetics as they quaffed their Chiot wine to the health of their orthodox and beloved lady, Theodora. And do not imagine, dear reader, that these were fantasies on the part of excited monks or the ravings of the chroniclers; on the contrary, they are actual miracles and recognized by the Church and, as such, every Orthodox Christian must, according to the canon of the Holy Ecumenical Council of Nicaea "accept them on faith wholeheartedly", whilst should he dare to "doubt them as impossible or misinterpret them as he sees fit, *anathema sit*!"

While the ascetics were talking of miracles, Nicetas was discussing with the two Benedictines and the Byzantine eunuchs concerning doctrine. First of all, he asked Joan what the divines of the West believed concerning Holy Communion, if, that is, they believed that the bread and wine were truly changed into the body and blood of the Saviour or whether they considered it a symbol and image of the divine body. This question was of great concern to the clerics of the time just as the Eastern Question is today. Not knowing her host's views on the matter, Joan gave a diplomatic answer, saying that the sun is in the sky while its light and warmth are on the earth and similarly the body of Christ seated at the right hand of the Father is also found in the Communion bread and wine. Yet this metaphysical answer did not please Nicetas who, believing in the "actual presence", explained to Joan that the bread and wine are the dead body of Christ, our stomach his tomb, in which he is buried by the priest, but before long he rises out of this, just as, following the Crucifixion, Jesus rose from the tomb on the third day. After this, he asked her whether Christians in the West also honoured the Virgin with the epithet "Mother of God" or "Deipara". Joan replied that the hen was called "ovipara" and the cat "vivipara", so they were afraid lest the word "deipara", because of its similarity, scandalize the faithful and, in addition, they did not wish to provide the pagans with an excuse to identify the Mother of God with Rhea, as did the followers of Hypatia in Egypt. Then, wanting herself to test the Bishop, she asked him why the Eastern Christians did not cut their hair, going against the counsel of St. Paul, who considered it effeminate and improper for a man to have long hair.[20] Having no answer to this,[21] Nicetas scratched his hairy head and once again turned the discussion back to doctrinal matters concerning the "antidosis" or dual nature of Jesus following his incarnation, whether the Logos united with the body of the Saviour in the womb of the Virgin or after parturition,

---

[20] I Corinthians 11, 14-15: "…if a man hath long hair, it is a shame unto him; but if a woman have long hair, it is a glory to her."

[21] Most probably there is some logical answer, but I am unable to find it. The priests whom I asked about this had not even heard of Nicetas.

and other knotty theological problems, which the Church Fathers in Ephesus had solved by the sword, as Alexander the great had done with the Gordian knot, or by kicking, as asses do their mating and grazing differences.[22]

Presently night began to fall and the deacons in attendance hastened to fetch lamps to illuminate their Bishop's discussions so that he would not find himself in obscurity like the Holy Fathers who had abolished the icons at the time of the Emperor Constantine the Copronymus. But the guests, already weary of that perplexing discussion, abandoned the arguments and returned again to their cups. Dizzy from the wine and the cries of the surrounding monks, who were already teaching the platters to dance and the cups to fly, Joan got up quietly and left the bishopric, followed by the faithful Frumentius.

The garden was, as we said, on the slopes of the Acropolis, so after only a short climb, the two lovers found themselves atop that marble rock, concerning which some adherent to "final causes" might say that it was placed there deliberately in order to serve as a pedestal for the monuments of Pericles, just as, according to them, the nose was placed in the middle of

---

[22] According to Evagrius (Book II, Ch. 2), Flavian, the Patriarch of Constantinople, was removed during the Second Council of Ephesus and kicked by Dioscorus, the Patriarch of Alexandria, who, according to the testimony of Zonaras (Book 13, p. 44), had the bad habit of kicking like a mule.

the face in order to support a pair of spectacles. It was
that time of night when the vampires, the undead, the
lamias and other creatures of the dark escape from the
worms of the grave or the gates of Hades, given that
these are no longer guarded by the three-headed
Cerberus, and roam in the fields, disturbing the
dreams of sheep and the kisses of lovers. Yet our
monks, having one of St. Sabine's teeth hanging round
their necks, were for this reason able to avoid any evil
encounters; only from afar did they see a band of ass-
headed spirits who, shaking their long ears, were gazing amorously at the moon, in the light of which they
were seeking the awaited Messiah. Two or three times
they tripped over monks sleeping on the slabs of the
Propylaea and who never even moved, because the
Greeks were already used to being trodden on like
grapes under the feet of foreigners. Joan had never
seen any temples other than the Druids' monoliths
and some formless Roman ruins, while in her homeland, most of the churches were wooden and rough
like those constructed by the Germans, with the result
that she could not get her fill of gazing in wonder at
the columns of the Parthenon and the Caryatids of the
Erechtheum, about which Frumentius, kissing their
feet, asked if they were petrified angels. The Temple of
Parthena Athena belonged at that time to the Virgin
Mary. Yet at that moment neither nasal chanting
nor the mournful fumes of incense nor the annoying
chiming of bells came to disturb the charms of their
musings. There were but a few owls nesting in the cav-

ities in the roof that occasionally let out a plaintive cry as if they were lamenting their mistress' exile. The disc of Hecate, surrounded by transparent clouds like some demure maiden in her night attire, shone motionless at an unfathomable height, pouring down over those immortal marbles a white and pale light, like that over the sleeping Adonis, when he was visited by the goddess on the peak of Mount Latmus. The columns of the Temple of Olympian Zeus, the stream of the Illyssos, the blue waves of the Bay of Phaleron, the olive groves, the oleanders, the hilltops crowned with churches or monuments all girdled the sight of the young couple with a girdle even more alluring than Aphrodite's. The delight that they felt at this panorama was doubled because, being drunk, they saw everything double. Joan had sat down on a marble seat, while Frumentius, leaning against his beloved's legs, was pointing out to her the Temple of Wingless Victory, hoping that their love would remain wingless like this was. So speaking and often punctuating their words with kisses, as writers do their sentences with commas, they fell asleep on the Pentelic marble as Jacob had on the stones of Harran.

The next morning, shaking the sleep from their eyes and the dew from their cassocks, they went down to see the city of Athens. Joan's heart was pounding out of curiosity and apprehension at the thought that she would soon be marvelling at that idolatrous city, of which the sight alone, according to St. Gregory, was dangerous for Christian souls, just as the sight of a former pretty and delightful mistress is to a man married to an ugly and scowling wife. Yet the hopes and fears of our heroine proved groundless. For long before, the pious Byzantine emperors had torn down the works of Myron, Alcamenes and Polykleitos, which St. Luke had marvelled at and Alaric had respected. The work of destruction begun by Constantine had been brought to completion by Theodosius the Younger. And it was not only against the stones that these tireless idol-destroyers showed such Christian zeal, but also against those poor wretches who were suspected of adhering to the religion of their ancestors. Anyone slaughtering a lamb for a family feast or laying flowers at his father's tomb or gathering chamomile under the moonlight or perfuming his house or wearing a talisman round his neck against fever was denounced by hooded spies as a wizard or idolater, bound in chains and sent to Scythoupolis, where the Christian slaughterhouse had been set up. There, pious judges convened and vied with each other as to who would roast on the gridiron or boil in burning oil or dismember the most idolaters. There are thousands of testimonies recounting the deeds of the Christian martyrs, from whose wounds dripped milk and who were fanned by the flames, but no one has yet written the indisputable Legendary of those martyrs who, instead of mythical milk, shed real blood and, instead of being fanned, were incinerated by the flames of Christian intolerance, being even more caustic, it seems, than the fire of polytheistic brutality.

The two Benedictines, followed by Theonas and a crowd of Athenians who, just as during the time of the Apostle, "had time for nothing else save to listen to or relate some news", wandered through the entire city which, deprived of its idols and altars, resembled Polyphemus after being blinded by Odysseus. Where previously a statue had stood, they had set up a wooden cross, and where an altar had been, a tiny church with a domed roof resembling a stone wig. These tiny churches had been constructed by the Athenian Eudocia who, wishing to dedicate a special abode to each of the saints, was obliged to build a plethora of huts, which recalled the building technology of beavers rather than the magnificence of the unknown god. At their doorways sat monks and ascetics, scratching their sores or ancient manuscripts in order to write the lives of saints, weaving baskets, breakfasting on onions and perhaps themselves thanking God that they had been born Greeks and not barbarians. The only thing for the two foreigners to marvel at was the archaic beauty of the women. During that century, Athens was a source of women for the Byzantine Emperors, from where they chose their wives, just as their successors, the Sultans, did from Circassia. This improvement in the Attic race began from the time of the iconomachy, when, given that the Byzantine icons were banished, the women, instead of constantly having before their eyes scrawny madonnas or scraggy saints, raised their eyes once again to the bas reliefs of the Parthenon and bore children like to these; so that also from the point of view of eugenics, I consider the transformation of our ecclesiastical iconography a necessity. Proof of the influence of images is provided by the wives of the Jewish bankers in Prussia, who from morning to night count pieces of silver and gold bearing the head of King Wilhelm and bear children so like the king that he is rightly called father of his people.[23] Yet apart from the beauty of the women, the two children of the North also marvelled at what to them was unusual demureness on the part of the maidens, who, wrapped in their long robes, kept close to their mother's side as a sword to a soldier's thigh, while their gazes, instead of returning the looks of the passers-by, were fixed on the ground, thereby avoiding both potholes and improprieties. They would blush whenever the breeze caught hold of the hems of their garments and in everything they were totally different from the girls of today, who so resemble married women that one wonders why their fathers seek husbands for them. After passing the Tower of the Winds and the marketplace, where they saw and marvelled at the gentry and bishops shopping for their daily greens, they arrived at the Poikile Stoa, which was no longer the place of philosophers but of astrologers, fortune-tellers, dream-interpreters and the schoolteachers, who came down there once a week from their schools on Hymettus in order to attract pupils by their eloquence and by pots of

---

[23] See Henrich Heine, *Reisebilder*, vol. 2.

Hymettus honey; since to their teaching, which was no longer sufficient for their needs, they had added, in order to earn a living, apiculture, just as the monks in Florence also add to the profits from their liturgies those of viniculture.

Joan, together with her companion, spent ten whole days visiting the antiquities, the churches and the environs of Athens, and another ten were spent resting under the hospitable roof of the Monastery of Daphne. The monks there were ready to offer lifelong hospitality to the two Benedictines, whose descendents would soon drive them from their fold like preying wolves.[24] But the tasteless diet, the long prayers, the straw pallets and the filthiness of the goodly fathers made it impossible for these children of the west to be happy there for very long, accustomed as they were in the more relaxed monasteries of Germany to eating and washing every day. So, forsaking the glory of the Major Orders and of the Angelic followers of St. Basil and finding harsh the rules of even the Minor Orders, they adhered themselves with the "Idiorhythmics",[25] at whose own discretion it was left to attain a higher or lower place in Paradise by means of more or less

---

[24] The Monastery of Daphne was in fact, at the time of the Dukes of Laroche, taken over by the Benedictines, whose tombs can still be seen in the entrance to the Church. See Rangavis, *Hellenica*, vol.1, p.221.

[25] Concerning the differences between these Orders, see the clarifications by Leo Allatius (*De Consensus Ecclesiae Vol. 3*, ch.8) and the *Confessionale* by Nicodemus, p.162.

prayers or penances, or to go freely to Hell, if they loved their neighbour and wine and good meat. At a short distance from the monastery was a hermitage that was empty owing to the death of the hermit St. Hermylus who, attempting not to take any food other than the Holy Eucharist, had died after following this diet for ten days. Here is where the two lovers built their nest, spending their small fortune on the purchase of a thick mattress, a small spit, a copper pot, a jug of oil, two goats, ten hens and a big dog in order to guard all these; while the tools necessary for the salvation of their souls—a whip, a skull and a good example—they inherited from the deceased.

The first days after the two monks had moved there were a constant celebration. Lent had passed and Jesus had risen from the dead; from everywhere came the sound of kissing and the lambs had returned to the roasting spit, while nature itself, as though wishing to celebrate the resurrection of the Saviour, shook off her winter garb like a young widow her mourning for her husband. Apollo's laurels were turning red, the grass was sprouting amidst the ruins and the spring was teaching the asses to dance with their mates. Rising with the dawn, Joan joyfully breathed in the early morning mountain breezes, milked the goats —given that the law had not yet come into force which prohibits milking by monks as giving rise to wicked desires—gathered fresh cherries, boiled eggs and then woke Frumentius. After breakfast, he would go to catch fish or set traps for the hares, while Theonas tended to the garden and Joan, withdrawing into the recesses of her cell, sometimes wrote out the lives of the saints, which she sold to increase the household income, or sometimes spent the day reading the dreams of Plato or the sighs of Theocritus in manuscripts which were lent to her or given to her by the monks, like the fox in the fable gave barley to the horse. In the evening, supper was taken in front of the hermitage door under an old pine tree, which the villagers called "the Patriarch" because of its height and age; while the products of the garden, of fishing and of hunting rendered the table of the two monks, who as Saxons and Benedictines had healthy appetites, unique on that hill. Reading day and night Greek philosophers and sometimes eastern ones or heretical Church Fathers who had lived before the invention of fasting, dogma and hymns, Joan had gradually scraped away the monkish rust from upon her. Being by nature sagacious and skeptical, she fashioned a kind of tolerant religion of her own, very similar to the systems of her modern countrymen, who, thanks to enlightened progress and the theological schools of Berlin and Tübingen, have succeeded in creating a form of Christianity without Christ, just as some refined chefs managed to produce garlic sauce without garlic and Mr P. Soutsos poems without poetry. Frumentius, being ready like the heroes of the romantic school to share heaven or hell with his beloved, ate chicken with her on Fridays and lamb on Wednesdays. In Rome, whenever a dictator was being elected, all other jurisdictions would cease; so also when love is rendered the absolute ruler, all other feelings fade in the heart like stars in the sky when the sun rises. Forgetting his divinity, Zeus would adorn himself with wings or horns in order to please his mistresses. Aristotle, wearing a saddle on his back and a bridle over his mouth, offered his seventy year-old body to Cleophile for her to use like asses are used in India. So Frumentius would not only have eaten meat on Fridays, but would have eaten anything served up to him for the sake of Joan.

The aromas from that impious kitchen scandalized more than a little the pious nostrils of the Greek monks. Many of them, passing outside the hermitage, would make the sign of the cross and cover their noses, just as Odysseus had covered the ears of his companions that they might not hear the song of the Sirens; while others, slightly more daring, went there to frighten our two flesh-eating monks with the flames of hell or excommunication from the Church. But Joan welcomed them all with such kindness and offered them the largest portion with such joy that these "Major Order" monks, followers of St. Basil, who ate nothing with wings save for the flies that fell into their insipid broth, would often come out with turtle dove in their bellies and sins on their conscience.

Meanwhile, word of the sagacity, the comeliness and the knowledge of the young "brother John" spread throughout the hills and began to filter down into the city too. Leaving their bees and their pupils, many of the erudite teachers of Mt. Hymettus journeyed to visit our heroine in order to converse with her on thorny problems of doctrine or on demons and fortune-telling; even the archbishop Nicetas would come often to rest under the shade of the giant pine tree, marvelling like Petrarch at how the fruit of knowledge could so quickly ripen under the fair locks of that twenty year-old head. Yet it was not only the priests and the savants, but also the nobles and passing patricians of New Rome who eventually came to learn the way to the hermitage. No one passed through Daphne without knocking on the door of the Benedictines; while many, on seeing the tender arms or kissing the white fingers of "Father John", were overcome by some inexplicable agitation, as if their heart had been pricked by the demon of sensuality. Thinking that her male attire was safe armour against all evil desires and unaware of the customs of those Neoplatonists, Joan generously exuded the smell of incense, each day yoking to her cart some new admirer of her boundless wisdom and her rosy lips. Often, surrounded by such a crowd, she reflected with a sigh how many more ardent admirers she would have, if, instead of hiding her charms beneath a cassock like a golden blade in a lead scabbard, she were to suddenly reveal herself in her true form, wearing a silk dress and with her fair hair falling over her shoulders. Yet the poor young girl was ignorant of the fact that, were this to happen, most of those eastern Christians would turn their backs, as Lucian's heroine did to her beloved ass when it was transformed into a man.

At first, Frumentius was happy at his sweetheart's good fortune, but he soon began to notice in Joan's behaviour certain changes, which alarmed him, as the first wrinkles do a coquette. Under that robust and virile exterior, the young monk concealed a heart softer than a fig, born to love as a nightingale to sing and an ass to kick. And though he was capable of swallowing two hundred chestnuts without feeling the slightest stomach ache, from his sweetheart he was unable to digest even so much as a yawn or a cool look; and this was after seven years of constant conjugal living! According to the moralists, pleasure is the death of love; whereas I would compare it rather to the breath of that Aesopian satyr which sometimes blows warm and sometimes cold. Yet, without any doubt whatsoever, the kisses and caresses of our heroine had become as necessary to the goodly Frumentius as his daily bread, and as these grew less, so his appetite increased as though he had been deprived of part of his daily diet. The months and the years passed and Joan became ever more distant as the circle of her admirers grew, while the despondency of the poor young man increased every day and a pale cloud spread over his young cheery face like a black veil over a flowering rosebush. For a long time he tried to conceal his impatience like the Spartans did the fox tearing at their flesh, but in the end the tears flowed from his eyes and the grievances from his lips. At first, Joan tried to console her companion, certain that the gloomy clouds surrounding him were nothing more than dark moths, creations of his fevered mind. But Frumentius was inconsolable, while women soon tire of despondency. Even the Oceanids, though goddesses, stayed no more than one day to comfort the bound Prometheus before growing tired of his grieving and leaving him on the rock with the eagle devouring his innards. So too our heroine. After offering some comfort to her companion and occasionally a hasty kiss, as one may toss a coin into the hand of a poor beggar, she then turned her back on him first at night, that she might sleep, and then during the day that she might keep company with her books and her admirers, whose visits followed one after the other from morning to night. Frumentius usually stayed in some corner of the room, brooding like Homer's heroes. Sometimes he felt it impossible to hold back his tears or his temper and he would rush out of the house to pluck a chicken for supper or a daisy to discover whether or not Joan loved him.

But such a state of affairs could not continue indefinitely. The young monk sometimes thought of cutting off Joan's head and sometimes of cutting off his relations with her. Our heroine's coquetry and flirtatiousness "assumed a greater significance with each new day", as the journalists would put it. One abbot, two archbishops and the Prefect of Attica already knew the content of her cassock, while many others harboured suspicions and the rest offered the incense of Platonic worship to brother John; while Frumentius did not stop grousing or reviling his sweetheart who, eventually losing her patience, answered him in a manner as dry as the figs of Kalamata. The relationship between the young couple had gradually come to resemble those Indian fig trees surrounding our Royal Gardens, whose fruit lasts one day and whose thorns last all year. Meanwhile, whenever Frumentius thought of separating from his beloved, he felt his hair stand on end in horror. The poor lad was unable to live either with or without her. Unaware that the heart of a woman is like moving sand on which one can pitch camp only for one night, he had constructed his house there, intending to live all his life in it. Driven out of that Eden with kicking and cursing, he did not succumb like Adam to his punishment, but kept on seeking ways to once again enter that forbidden garden whose gate was shut to him by Joan's indifference and meanness just as Paradise was to Adam by the angel's sword. Sometimes he would fall at his beloved's feet and he would try to move her, reminding her of all the kisses and vows, but his words slid off her callousness like rain off leaves; sometimes roaming in the woods like a wounded deer, he would look for a magic wand to use it to make a few tears run from Joan's dry eyes like Moses did water from the rock in the desert. There were times, too, when, no longer having any hope, he sought to uproot the love from his heart as a gardener might uproot a smelly onion from a patch of sunflowers; but this annoying plant had deep roots so that, abandoning his efforts after vain struggles, he would fall to the ground, covered in sweat and like Job cursing "the day on which he had been born and the hour he had been pronounced a male."

Yet do not imagine, dear reader, that the goodly Frumentius had become a lovesick youth or one of Mr. Soutsos' heroes or some similar form of bipod from the romantic menagerie; on the contrary, he was a sensible and devoted child of heroic Germany, like those born of that classical land of beer and sausages before it was corrupted by the sighs of Werther and the blasphemies of Strauss and Hegel, and he loved Joan as perhaps Aristippus did Laïs and cats do milk. But apart from her, he knew no other woman nor was it possible for him to find one in Athens; for the descendants of Solon were not yet, as today, civilized, while mothers, husbands, brothers and other such troublesome beings, who surrounded their women as thorns do roses, did not yet question the honour of holding a candle for foreigners, whether admirals or diplomats. In fact, the Athenian women of that time held out a hand only to the Byzantine Emperor, and even to them only the right hand. All this rendered poor Frumentius' position even more difficult and his follies excusable, since for someone like him at the height and fullness of his youth, a woman was an indispensible aid just as crutches are for the lame and manure for the fields. It is in distant lands and mythical ages that the poets and fabulists place their strange and monstrous creations of the vegetable or animal world, honeyed lotuses, singing trees, winged dragons, goat-legged satyrs, hydras, giants, sirens, heroes, wizards, prophets, martyrs, saints and other such beings, the likes of which not one of us has ever seen other than in depiction or in dream. Yet the moral realm too, if you would forgive me this expression, dear reader, also has its mythology, heroic devotion, pious ecstasy, superhuman sacrifice, inseparable friendship and other suchlike dramatic or fictional content. Among these chimerical products of past times, we should, I believe, also assign love, as this was understood by the medieval knights and the misinterpreters of Plato, whereas to a healthy philosophy it is no more than the "contact of two epidermises".[26] Even if Frumentius was ready to do anything for Joan's sake, even if, rolling at her feet, he cursed the day he was born, he did all this for the same reason that Adam forgave his faithless wife, namely... that he had no one else.

Yet our heroine, too, though encircled by devotees, was far from resting on a bed of roses. Though Frumentius' wailing and lamentations no longer moved her, nevertheless they got on her nerves and often affected her sleep or her appetite, and even worse, revealed the couple's secret to everyone. According to Athenaeus, dear reader, love and a cough are the only things that cannot be concealed. In my opinion (if that is I am permitted to voice an opinion contrary to those of the inebriated deipnosophists), there is nothing more easily concealed than love, unlike a cough,

---

[26] This brilliant definition belongs to Samfort.

whenever this happens. Only jealousy, anxiety, desperation and similar amorous accoutrements are imprinted on the face like the blows of the executioner, while joy and happiness are granted to us so sparingly by the daughters of Eve that they may be easily hidden beneath a monk's cassock or even in the pocket of a tight waistcoat. All women, without exception, resemble those brutal Romans in the age of decline, who demanded of the victims slaughtered in the amphitheatre that they fall with grace, gladly offering their necks to the sword. So too Joan, after variously tormenting poor Frumentius through jealousy, indifference, caprices and other female devices, then became enraged at him should a cry of grief escape from his lips amidst all these torments or should he, in his despair, show his teeth or the hermitage door to one of his rivals for her love.

Meanwhile, the scandalous goings-on in the hermitage caused a stir among all the cowled inhabitants in the area, for whom Joan—and no one was any longer in doubt as to her sex or her indiscretions—was a monster sent by the Franks to devour the Orthodox Church. And it is true that many women before her, such as St. Matrona, St. Pelagia and St. Macrina, had donned the cassock and lived among monks, but what they had not done was to eat turtle doves and lead bishops astray. Among this enraged band were a few monks who endeavoured to defend the fair German girl, but their voices were drowned amid the general outcry. Those who were most furious with her were some "angelic First-Order" monks, who were foul-smelling and filthy like all those wishing to please God alone. Endeavouring at every opportunity to ingratiate themselves with Joan, they were summarily sent by her to the baths and the barber. Thus they were now taking revenge on this ungracious nun by hurling curses and anathemas at her whenever she emerged from her cell and sometimes even onions, like the noble youths of Athens do at the chanteuses of the Italian Theatre, whenever these Italian nightingales find their sighs annoying or their gifts inadequate.

Thus beset from within by Frumentius and from without by common opinion, and seeing that the zeal of her followers was growing less each day out of fear of anathema at the same time that the boldness of her enemies was ever increasing, Joan began to think seriously about leaving. She had been in Athens for eight whole years and knew everything about the monuments there, the manuscripts and the inhabitants, so that the city of Athens already seemed as tiresome to her as the kisses of Frumentius. And, in addition to this, she was consumed by the desire to display her learning, her beauty and her wit on a bigger stage, already approaching the thirtieth year of her life; an age when women, no longer content with their own particular failings, are wont to adorn themselves with ours, acquiring ambition, fastidiousness, inebriety and whatever other "male" vice might render their hearts a model of female perfection, just as, today, Greece's politicians have rendered it a model of an Oriental kingdom. Joan was nothing like those shepherdesses of Ovid, who were content if Athos simply listened to their songs or if the stream reflected their garlanded faces, but, on the contrary, she would often weep over her books, reflecting that her wisdom would remain unknown and unsung in that little corner of Attica, just as young nuns weep when, disrobing at night, they reflect that their lily-white and alluring limbs are seen only by their incorporeal and invisible bridegroom. It was in such a mood that she found herself when, one evening while she was wandering along the curved shore of Piraeus, where she had gone to bid farewell to her friend Nicetas, who was returning to Constantinople, she noticed a foreign ship entering the port. Its white sails seemed to her like the wings of an angel coming to free her from her place of exile. The ship was Italian, belonging to Guglielmo Minimus, Bishop of Genoa, and coming from the East to procure incense for His Eminence and uniforms for his servants. Shouting in Latin to the disembarking sailors, Joan discovered that they would leave the next morning for Rome and that they were willing to take her to replace the priest who had been sailing with them but who had been taken by the waves while standing in the prow and attempting, as is the custom of the Catholics, to calm the storm by throwing into the sea some holy crusts which served as communion for the dolphins. Agreeing to all this, Joan returned to Frumentius, who was waiting for her in a nearby grotto in the bay of Mounichia, where he had prepared their supper and bed. The weather was damp, the wind bitter and the sea sighed mournfully beneath the grotto. The young Benedictine hastened to light a fire, beside which Joan sat in order to dry her clothes soaked by the waves. Her heart, though for a long time now hardened by her fastidiousness and coquetry, was filled with not a little anxiety when she reflected that soon she would part forever from her companion, from whom she had never once been separated during a span of fifteen years. For a few moments she thought of including him in her new wanderings; but the peculiar jealousy of the poor monk who cherished the musty idea that women should have only one lover like asses one saddle and peoples one king rendered him a troublesome and heavy burden. Yet nor did Joan dare to bid him farewell, fearful in that deserted place of his tears or even his fists. Therefore she considered it more merciful and at the same time more prudent to lull him to sleep in her arms rather like the executioners in Judaea offer some intoxicating potion to the condemned before crucifying them. So taking Frumentius' head in her lap, she began to run her fingers through his hair and to kiss his brow, while this guileless young man, so often cursed, deceived and abused, instantly forgot all the infidelities, the curses and the torments. Simply the touch of Joan's fingers healed all his wounds, just as, prior to the constitution, the French kings healed their subjects' sores by a simple laying-on of hands. Filled with indescribable bliss, Frumentius did not know which of all the saints to thank for this sudden change, for in his despair he had called upon all of them, and not having slept for a long time, he finally fell asleep on that sweetest of pillows, promising to chant hymns and light candles to all of them.

When the next morning, before even daybreak, he opened his arms to embrace his beloved, instead of her, all he embraced was the straw of her pallet. Leaping up in alarm, he reached out his arms and fumbled in the dark like the blind Polyphemus searching for Odysseus. The light of dawn was still struggling against the darkness when, bareheaded, barefoot and desperate, the poor young man emerged from the grotto, but there was no trace of Joan. After several times scouring the hill to no avail, he rushed down to the shore leaping from crag to crag like a wild boar and shouting "Joan!" in a loud voice. The hollow rocks echoed his cry so that however many times Frumentius shouted, they too shouted after the runaway girl, as though pitying the wretched boy; while at that moment even the sun came up to help in his desperate search. But the shore was deserted, while a rowing boat could be seen on the sea, riding the waves of Mounichia, and in its prow stood Joan, wrapped in her robe. Perhaps the runaway saw the young man on the shore waving his arms to her and then leaping into the sea, but she only turned her head, urging the rowers to go faster.

Presently, the rowing boat came up alongside the ship, which unfurled its sails to the wind, while Frumentius, after his vain pursuit, with his hopes and strength exhausted, fell like a breathless shipwreck on the quayside. When he came round, he repulsed life like a bad dream. Yet the hours passed, the sun dried his clothes and his dream did not come to an end. For a moment he thought of drowning it in the sea as Solomon had drowned his sorrows in wine, but the water was shallow and, in addition, he was fearful of Hell, where he would still have to wait a long time for Joan. Then he lifted his grieving gaze to Heaven, but not one of the female saints there came down to offer her lips in consolation as Bacchus had done for Ariadne. Besides, Frumentius was not a woman, and who knows if, in the mood he was in, he would have cursorily pushed away even St. Thaïs or the fair Magdalen?

When night fell, he returned once again to the grotto. What sort of night can he have spent there facing the pallet on which Joan's comely shape was still visible in the depression she had left imprinted there? If, dear reader, you have ever lost a lover or an entire fortune at cards, you will be able to imagine; or if you have ever drunk absinth after a meal, you will know just how bitter the tears were that he shed. He remained there two whole weeks, asking "Wherefore is light given to him that is in misery, and life unto the bitter in soul."[27] But finally, pitying him, Boniface, his patron saint in Heaven, came to his aid. One evening while Frumentius was sleeping on the shore, having exhausted all his lamentations, this apostle of the Saxons

---

[27] Job 3, 20.

came down from Heaven, opened the sleeping youth's breast with a knife, inserted his holy fingers into the opening and, pulling out his heart, plunged it into a pool of water, which he had previously sanctified. The burning heart writhed in the water like whitebait in the frying pan and, after it had cooled, the saint put it back again in its rightful place and, closing the wound, returned to his own rightful place.

Has it ever happened to you, dear reader, to fall asleep with an insufferable cough, to sweat all night while asleep and to wake up cured? Unaware that you are better, you mechanically open your mouth in order to pay the usual toll to the accursed cough. Yet what joy you feel in no longer finding the annoying beast in your throat! So too Frumentius, on opening his eyes and getting ready to offer to the ungrateful Joan the usual libation of tears, found against all expectations his eyes to be dry and this goodly Benedictine had a desire not for weeping but for breakfasting after so many days of going without food. Presently, a young shepherdess passed before him carrying a jug of milk on her head and a string of bread rolls. Calling her over, he dined happily. When this Amaryllis, accepting a copper coin and kissing the monk's hand, walked off, her joyous song merged with the voice of the larks while the morning breeze played with the folds of her dress, lifting it above her calves. On seeing her, Frumentius realized for the first time that there were other women in the world apart from Joan. His cure then could now be considered complete. Thus, by virtue of the saint's miracle, he was stripped of his foolish passion and rendered useless as the hero of our novel, whereas, on the contrary, from that moment he became a most useful member of society, capable, were he to be living today, of practising any respectable occupation, of becoming a postman, a spy, a politician, a fortune-hunter or office-seeker, of keeping the ledgers of a Chiot merchant or holding the feet of a hanged convict. But in those times, chanting the "Lord have mercy" was the best kind of trade, so Frumentius did the right thing to remain a monk as before. But now I wish to rest awhile before chasing after Joan to Rome. Great poets, like Homer and Mr P. Soutsos, write wonderful verses in their sleep, but I always dry my pen before putting on my nightcap. It is only notable men who are forgiven somnolent sentences, while we humble scribes have always to remain "awake" like the Capitoline geese that awakened the Romans.

Part IV

"Φεύ της θηλείας, πη προβήσεται, φρένος,
Τι τέρμα τόλμης και θράσους γενήσεται?"[1]
(Euripides, *Hippolytus* 935)

The cradle of all great men is shrouded in the deepest darkness, into which only poets and fablers dare venture by lighting their imagination's magic lantern, in the light of which they see myriads of pale and smiling phantoms. Yet once the hero has come of age and the blossom has put forth fruit, there comes a swarm of historians wielding the blazing and radiant torch of criticism. At the appearance of these glowering torchbearers, the golden-winged creatures of imagination flee in fear, since, like the stars and forty-year old women, they are happy only in the dimness; whereas, if the light is too bright, the hero often disappears before the critic's eyes as Homer before the eyes of Wolf

---

[1] Trans. note: "Ah the female mind! Say, how far will it go? / What end is there to its boldness and audacity?" The original has "mortal mind".

and Jesus before those of Strauss. Yet Joan remained unshakeable in that lofty position, in no way daunted by the light; but henceforth she becomes a historical figure and the delicate garlands with which I adorned the fair locks of the seventeen year-old girl are no longer seemly on the head that is soon to be adorned by the triple crown of St. Peter. Consequently, instead of drawing the material for my narration from out of my head as before, I am from now on obliged to resort to the eminent chroniclers, so if you find this part of the book less palatable, dear reader, I thank you for your preference.

Having lost the world it had conquered by the sword, Rome was busy reestablishing its empire, now sending doctrines in place of legions to its erstwhile provinces and quietly weaving that vast web in which it would enmesh all nations. When our heroine arrived in Rome, the spider in that web was St. Leo IV, successor to Sergius, surnamed "Bocca di Porco" or "Pigmouth". In those times, virtually all the prelates, whether they wanted to or not, received the title of saint, but this Leo, by virtue of his own sweat, was truly deserving of it for having found the bodies of the saintly martyrs Sebronius, Nicostratus and Castorius, for having created with his crosier, as Poseidon did with his trident, a terrible tempest to scatter the Saracen ships, for having killed with his words alone a terrifying dragon nesting in the Church of St. Lucia, for having repulsed on numerous occasions the forays of the heathens and, the most pleasing of all to God, for having founded within

the papal palace a nunnery, where, under his patron-
age, the choicest of Rome's maidens became hallowed.
And, in addition to being a patron of the nuns, the
cultured pontiff was also a patron of the arts, and he
was so taken with Joan that, after speaking with her for
a long time on all the familiar topics and many more
besides, he immediately appointed her master of Theology in the school of St. Martin, where the venerable
Augustine had once taught.

Joan, or rather "Father John" (for her female name,
already unpleasant to the ear, will be assigned to our
heroine only when we are alone with her, just as the
Emperor Alexander gave the title of "thief" to his ministers when in private), spent her first days wandering
through the "Eternal City". But the monuments of
Rome then were not worth even the wear and tear on
the shoes of those visiting them. Lord Elgin's tutor,
Charlemagne, had, in keeping with the Frankish custom, looted the ancient temples to adorn the metropo-
lis of Aachen with their columns and reliefs; while the
Christian churches built by Leo's predecessors were
disproportionate and monstrous mixtures of Roman
and Oriental design, much like to Christianity in the
West at that time, being an incoherent and indigestible
mixture of Judaism and paganism, which would be
later processed and cleansed by the French theologians,
just as their descendents did with the slag at Laurion.[2]

---

[2] Trans. note: The ancient mines of Laurion are best known for

But in those times no one was yet concerned about doctrines, while the ancient gods, at least those who had not been transformed into Christian saints, being exiled from Mt. Olympus, had taken up residence in Hades, where they lived in peace with the Devil of the Christians and the Satan of the Jews, had the recognition of the theologians, heeded the invocations of the magicians and sometimes even resided in the bodies of Christians, who were then called possessed. On the day of Joan's arrival, a strange ritual was being performed in Rome's churches in honour of the ancient gods. Bands of drunken Christians were dancing and chanting "sacrilegious" odes and crying "Euoi Euoi!" and chasing each other with whips like during the Saturnalia, while priestesses of Aphrodite, whose sole garment was a pendant round their neck and bells on their feet, were roaming through the crowds offering wine and kisses to the dancers in exchange for a few coppers and scandalizing the newly-converted foreigners in Rome, who assumed that all these things were part of the Christian liturgy, just as those present in some rowdy session of the American Congress might assume that kicking was part of democratic liberty.

These, then, were the people whom our heroine was going to cure with the salt of Attica. During the first

---

producing silver, but they were also a source of copper and lead. Abandoned in the first century BC, they were re-opened in 1864 by French and Greek companies and the ancient slag was reprocessed for its remaining lead and silver.

days, she endeavoured to speak to them of dogmatism, but her listeners considered these discussions concerning the nature of the Holy Trinity that so interested the Greeks to be as superfluous as the beards adorning their faces. The successors of the august Plato were still discussing in the East concerning the nature of God, but the descendants of Cato and Cincinnatus, being more practical, considered theology an important profession from which the priest expected his daily bread and, in addition, positions, bishoprics, horses, concubines and all those pleasant things that one acquires only through action and practical knowledge. So instead of investigating the mysteries of Heaven, these prudent people concerned themselves with spreading the Heavenly Kingdom throughout the world and in its name exacting taxes from all nations. Being by nature sagacious and wily like a serpent or woman, Joan quickly guessed her students' desires. So abandoning Byzantine ideologies, she hastened to descend from Heaven to earth and from the snowcapped peaks of metaphysics to the rich and fertile plains of Canon Law, lecturing eloquently the next day on the Pope's temporal authority, on Charlemagne's gift, on taxes, tithes, gold vestments and other priestly perks, by which the clerics try to render less unbearable their wait for Paradise, just as Penelope's suitors amused themselves with the servant girls while waiting to enjoy their mistress. By talking about such things, she eventually managed to win the favour of her audience, as Orpheus was able to charm even the stones with his lyre. The com-

parison is no exaggeration; for if they were not stones,
the Italians of the time were referred to by other nations at least as asses and their synods as asinine, while
the few teachers in Italy had been sent from
Ireland, Scotia and Galatia to the poor descendants
of Cicero just as today Hellenists are sent to us from
Germany. But Claudius, Dungall, Vigintimillus and the
other foreign savants were already dead or senile and,
in those dark ages, Italy surpassed its fellow nations in
ignorance as Calypso did her fellow nymphs in stature.
The majority of clerics were unable to read and, instead
of preaching the Gospels from the pulpit, recounted
fairytales to the faithful about how the Holy Virgin
with her lily-white hands supported the legs of hanged
criminals who had ever lit a candle before her icon;
about how in order to save a pious nun from sin she
had assumed her appearance on her bed and received
her lovers in her stead; about how those rejecting God
but remaining faithful to the Virgin were secretly led
by her into the heavenly abode and about how the merciful Mother of God provided pious lovers with philtres
and magical potions so that by means of these they
might win their beloved. Hearing all these things, the
Lombards, Franks, Burgundians and the other barbar-
ian neighbours of Italy despised the Pope's subjects so
much that the adjective "Roman" was for them more
insulting than any other insult, just as "Greek" for card
players has become a synonym for cheat.

The wisdom of our heroine shone in that deep
darkness like a lamp in the dimness of a gloomy night.

Large audiences, sometimes even Pope Leo himself, flocked to the Monastery of St. Martin to listen to this new Augustine, who, instead of dealing with the fearful mysteries of religion, spoke only of delightful and useful things, praising the virtues of the Pontiff and vilifying the Byzantines, explaining the theorems of Aristotle or telling of his descendants' wretchedness, garlic, sores and fasting. Joan's discourses resembled those hospitable establishments in Hamburg in which can be found food suitable for all tastes, scents for every nose and women who speak all languages and satisfy all desires. Our heroine would often begin with the Divine Law and finish with the art of cooking. But, in those times, the products of the human mind were not yet arranged in ordered compartments like the reptiles in the display cases of the museum. The sole discipline was Theology, which like Briareos had a hundred arms and was all-embracing and which all fitted into the fair-haired head of our heroine.

For two years Joan continued to teach. She owed all her renown to her eloquence, for no one in Rome even imagined what treasures she had hidden beneath her cassock. All the faces of the monks there were shaven and only their noses stuck out from under their cowls. And gradually, in the intoxication of her vanity, she almost came to believe herself that she had been transformed into a man as Tiresias was into a woman. Frumentius had long been forgotten and our ambitious cleric was in no rush to choose his successor, having her mind on higher things. Our fair heroine was already dreaming of an abbot's cloak, a legate's asses, a bishop's mitre, sometimes even of a pope's golden slippers; while being a sensible woman, she placed lovers last on the list, just as sweets are kept for the end of the banquet. Yet rather than simply surrender to vain musings, she worked day and night for her own advancement, flattering the powerful, teaching, writing and composing hymns to Christ and the Pope with rhythmic and rhyming verses, which she was the first to introduce into Italy. But she also concerned herself with medicine and, according to some malicious tongues, with magic, forcing the evil spirits, in other words the former gods, Bacchus, Hera, Pan and Aphrodite, to leave behind the gates of darkness and run like faithful servants at her call.

Anyhow, the renowned Pope Leo, already old and suffering from rheumatism from the time he wanted to walk on water like St. Peter and received an unwanted bath, losing his mitre and a good part of his dignity, appointed "Father John" as his "private" secretary. At that time, apart from the officials in the Pope's court, there were not only private officers, but also private servants, private chefs, private Ethiopians, private valets and floor sweepers. But also inside the Vatican there were private staircases and doors and rooms. In fact, often, Christ's representative on earth even held private dinners there, though I could not say whether he had the Apostles sitting at his table. When she first entered the private chambers of His Holiness, our heroine hardly dared set foot on those thick Oriental carpets, on which one might wish to glide like the horses of Erichthonius, the hooves of which barely touched the tips of the flowers when they galloped. When she arrived before the Ruler of all Christendom, who was seated on a gold and crimson throne, amidst silver canisters, solid gold gabatha,[3] censers inlaid with emeralds and other artifacts, she was so dazzled by the glare that, had she needed to spit, she would have dared to do so only in the wrinkled face of the Holy Father, finding no other place more grimy in that gleaming chamber. But instead of this, she bent her knee and piously kissed Leo's sandals, who, raising "Father John" with paternal tenderness, worked with him till the evening and was so pleased that from that day hence he would more easily deprive himself of attending mass than of being with his dear secretary.

The *cubiculari, dapipheri, ostiarii, scriptores, arcani*[4] and other courtiers surrounding Leo, who prided themselves on presenting His Holiness with their services, which slaves rendered to the Emperors of Rome, gossiped at first about the new favourite, like the bodyguards of the demure Catherine the Great, whenever any new candidate knocked on the door of her chamber. But the manner of "Father John" was so affable and gentle and he was so unselfish that before very

---

[3] Baronio, from whom this description was taken, uses the Greek word "gabatham" (porringer). Ann Ecles. Vol. I, p. 83.

[4] See the explanation of these terms in Muratori (*Antiquitates italicæ medii ævi*. Vol. VI).

long he won the hearts of all and all addressed themselves to him whenever they had something to ask of the Holy Father. Joan, being a stranger in Rome and not having the greed of either nieces or concubines to satisfy, readily hastened to submit her friends' petitions to the Pope, so that their number and gratitude grew day by day and very soon the private secretary became a veritable party leader, surrounded by a crowd of greedy toadies, who swarmed around her as hens around a farm maid shaking the grain from her apron.

While Joan took care of all her friends, she sought nothing for herself or, rather, what she wanted she dared ask for only from the Holy Virgin, begging the merciful Madonna to reward as quickly as possible the good works of the saintly Pope Leo by taking him to a better life. It was an ungrateful and impious wish to address to the Mother of God! But, in Rome, the faithful enjoy such familiarity with the Holy Virgin that they do not only ask her for riches, horses, positions and honours, but also the death of their enemies, of wealthy relatives, of rivals in love or of any other annoying beings, and other things too that would make even a procurer blush if asked of him. Murderers dedicated their knife on her altar before plunging it into the victim's innards; concubines stripping off their girdle hung it before her icon; and drunkards drained bottles and jugs in her name. Joan, being a clever woman, observed the local customs and so it was to the Virgin that she addressed her ambitious requests. Yet nor did she renounce the help of the Devil, and also had recourse to the horrible rites of medieval magic. Withdrawing to the ruins of an ancient temple, she invoked the evil spirits of the abyss, plunging a sharp needle into the breast of a wax image of Leo, while poisonous herbs burned in a tripod and the moon stood still, obeying the invocations of the magicians as the sun did those of Joshua.

I cannot say whether it was the Devil or the Holy Virgin that heeded our heroine's wishes, and nor did she know which of the two to thank, but it is a fact that Leo became ill before very long and his illness became worse day by day so that when the physicians had exhausted their potions and the monks their appeals to the archangel Michael, the successor to Asclepius, and the Jewish sorcerers and Arab astrologers had performed their arcane arts to no avail, it was decided by a general council of the bishops that the ruler of all Christendom should be transferred to the crypt of St. Tiburtius to await there the dream through which the saint would reveal to him the most suitable cure for his illness. In those times, the faithful in their perplexity had recourse to heaven-sent dreams, just as their ancestors had had recourse to the oracles of the Pythia and today's sick have recourse to the prescriptions of a medium's moving tables; while the church, though burning the fortune-tellers, accepted dream-interpretation, just as today the doctors condemn mesmerists yet make use of mesmerism.

The poor Pope, taken from his bed on a black stretcher, was carried by four sturdy monks to the crypt, where he was placed before the altar, surrounded by burning candles, desperate physicians and chanting priests. This laudable Pontiff, though a saint, was never overly pious and had spent his life beautifying Rome, amassing treasure, erecting more ramparts than churches and defending his territories against the Saracens rather than against the Devil, burning no heretics, but murdering many enemies so that, as Voltaire himself admits, he was more worthy of the title of a great king than of a saint. If, sometimes, he was obliged to work miracles, he did this as a favour to his foolish subjects as Jesus did for the Jews. But illness transforms even lions into hares and skeptics into pious Christians. Byron, the greatest poet of the century, whose brain weighed six hundred and thirty-eight drams, openly admits that when ill, following his first phlebotomy, he came to believe in the miracles of Moses, following the second, in the Incarnation, following the third, in the immaculate conception, and following the fourth, he was sorry that there were no more such things to believe in. So, too, the goodly Leo, perhaps the wisest man of his age, awaited his cure from St. Tiburtius. For three whole days the Pontiff remained without eating or moving, waiting for the arrival of the divine dream. But the pains would not allow him either to enjoy sleep or have any dreams and when, after three days of anguish he finally closed his eyes, it was in that sleep without dreams that lasts forever.

When, after the usual rites, the body of the renowned Leo, washed in wine and oil, was surrendered to the worms to feast on; when the bells had ceased tolling and the tears had dried, the Prelates, the lower clergy, the emissaries of the Emperor, the dignitaries and the entire populace gathered in St. Peter's square to give thought to the election of the future keeper of the keys of Paradise. During the ninth century, the pope was not yet elected in the secrecy and darkness of the hieratical synod; there was no Conclave nor were there cardinals shut up within dark cells with each one voting for himself, till by hunger they were obliged to compromise their demands,[5] but the Pontiffs were elected out in the open, in the midday sun, with wine flowing in abundance and blood too on many occasions, with the various factions competing with clubs and rocks more than with intrigue. In those times, the pope represented the people as the tribunes did the ancient Romans and so it was the people who had a major say in the choice of their representative. Votes were openly bought in exchange for promises, gold, wine or women, who wandered through the marketplace loosely clad, exchanging kisses for votes. Consequently, the death of the pope was a great joy for his subjects, who, just as the democratic peoples today, had as their only possession their vote, which with each new election gave even the common worker the

---

[5] According to the rule of the Lugdunum Synod, the Cardinals were shut in dark cells throughout the duration of the election. On the first day they were provided with two meals, on the second only one and for the rest of the time only with dry bread.

honour of shaking the hand of some wealthy ruler, of
drinking nectar from his gold cup and of resting on
the breast of his perfumed concubines. According
to St. Prudentius, there are certain days in Hades on
which the eternal fire is extinguished and the torments
of the condemned cease. Such days on earth for the
common people were and still are the days of the elec-
tions; the sole days on which it is remembered that the
servant and the lord, the clay cup and the decorated
cup, are similar vessels, moulded from the same clay
and by the same potter.

While the whole of Rome was gathering in the
square, our heroine, having long before arranged
everything in order to succeed in her ambitions, stood
in an upstairs room in the Monastery of St. Martin
and, with her hands crossed over her breast like
Napoleon, observed with an anxious gaze the changing fortunes of the electoral contest. That year there
were many contestants for the papal crown, but Joan's
four hundred students, the monks of her order, the
courtiers beholding to her, the female admirers of the
young Benedictine's comeliness and eloquence and
Leo's old adherents were all working on behalf of "Father John", lauding before the populace the wisdom,
the unselfishness and the virtues of their candidate,
who, being a foreigner without nephews or a harem,
would share St. Peter's revenue with the poor. The
struggle lasted four whole hours, during which time
Joan's face changed from one shade of colour to the
other, like the hands of the painters on the isle of

Syros, but already overcome by the emotion of it all, she sank upon a marble seat and, having closed her eyes, was awaiting her fate, when the joyous cries of her friends proclaiming Pope JOHN THE EIGHTH! awoke her from that anguished torpor. Reeling to and fro like the cottage of Isaiah,[6] the new Pontiff threw the purple cloak around her shoulders and donned the cross-bearing sandals, which, however, either because they were averse to women's feet or because they were too big, fell from her feet three times while she was descending the monastery steps. An enthusiastic crowd and a gold-trimmed mule was waiting by the door for the newly-proclaimed Pope, who, riding the mule, went immediately to the Lateran, where she sat on the golden throne and put on her head the triple crown of Rome, of the whole world and of Heaven, while the scribes wrote out the electoral decree amid the resounding acclamations of the crowds. To render the triumph of our heroine even more splendid, arriving in Rome on pilgrimage at that same moment was the King of England, Ethelwulf, who asked to be the first to kiss the new Pope's feet, rendering by this kiss all his lands subject to the Holy See; while at the same time emissaries from Constantinople presented themselves, bringing with them from the Emperor Michael precious gifts and together the cession of Syracuse. Joan at last saw the

---

[6] Isaiah 24, 20.

fulfillment of her youthful dreams;[7] she was sitting on a lofty throne and all around her were clouds of fragrant incense. Filled with indescribable joy, she turned her sparkling eyes to that kneeling crowd, then raising her gaze to the heavens, she cried: "Lioba, Lioba, thank you!"

The Master of Ceremonies interrupted the ecstasy of the newly-proclaimed Pope, inviting her to sit on a lowly chair, so-called "excremental", on which the Pontiff was placed following his inauguration so that he would remember that, though wearing a triple crown, he too was subject, like the least of his subjects, to the needs of his stomach. While His Holiness was sitting there, the priests chanted "and lifteth the needy out of the dunghill…", burning at the same time straw and oakum, in order to remind him that, just as that flame, so too the glory of this world fades and passes.

The ceremonies, feet-kissing and illuminations lasted for eight whole days. Yet while the deluded priests rubbed their lips on our heroine's sandals, the whole of nature rebelled against this sacrilege. On the day following the inauguration, though it was midsummer, all the roads of Rome were covered in a snowy blanket, as if the holy city wished to declare its mourning, donning its mournful winter attire like a funereal shroud. Yet in France and Germany too, there followed signs and wonders; earthquakes shook

---

[7] See p. 61.

the entire empire, while in Bresse it rained blood and in Normandy there was a hailstorm of dead locusts, the rotting bodies of which gave rise to a deadly plague. The owls and magpies nesting in the Vatican roofs screeched horribly for three whole nights, like the Capitoline geese when the Gauls threatened Rome. Who knows, if there had been moving tables at that time, these too might have raged and stamped their legs! I have listed all these signs related by reliable chroniclers in order to justify St. Peter who was unjustly condemned by the heretics for not hastening to defend his profaned see with some miracle. In addition to crows, plagues, blood and earthquakes, St. Peter could not use other signs against Joan because, according to Sirach, "Never good is any sign against a woman".[8]

When, after all these excitements, Joan finally remained alone in the enormous papal bedchamber, quiet, magnificent and fragrant as it was, she tried in vain to sleep in that purple bed, which resembled an altar built to Morpheus. Sorrow, joy and coffee have this same effect upon the eyelids. I very much doubt whether Alexander the Great, sleeping deeply on the day before I do not recall which battle, slept on the day after his victory. Yet why should we be seeking sleep and dreams when the truth, or "reality" as it is called

---

[8] *Super mulierum nunquam bonum est signum* (*Ecclesiasticus* XLVI, 6).

today, is sweeter than any dream? Who, with longing and emotion, does not recall the sleepless night passed after enjoying the riches of a lottery, the laurels of a poem or the position or wife of a close friend? Throwing off the gold-embroidered covers of the apostolic bed, she roamed barefoot in her new abode. Everywhere the light of her lamp was reflected in crystal, gold, turquoise and porphyry. The papal chamber resembled the paradise of St. John, who being a veritable Jew, aroused the avarice of his countrymen, describing the abode of the blessed as strewn with gold and diamonds. And this did more than a little to contribute to the spread of the Christian faith; for everyone preferred the precious Jewish paradise to the ancients' poor Elysian Fields, where instead of sapphires and pearls, there was nothing but groves of myrtles, limpid brooks and an ivory gate. Joan wandered through the chamber unable to have her fill of the sight of such treasures, weighing in her lily-white hands the jewelled cups, counting the diamonds and emeralds adorning the statue of the Virgin and examining the gems and wheels of the Arabian clock. Going over to a small table by the bed, on which a light meal had been prepared for Her Holiness should she wake during the night, she drank a cup of sweet Vesuvian nectar, Lacryma Christi, as the pious Italians had christened it, for a drop of which every true wine-drinker would gladly give a drop of his blood. The aroma of the wine mixed with the aroma of ambition heightened the intoxication of our heroine. If at that moment the chamberlain had appeared inviting her to sit on the "excremental" chair, or Philip's servant crying "Remember that you are mortal", she would have replied to both that they were animals. Finding the huge chamber too small for her greatness, she opened the window, from which she began to observe the city of Rome slumbering under the moonlight, in vain seeking to find another heroine in history worthy of comparison with her. Many women before her had girded the sword or placed the crown on their heads, but what are the withering laurels of war or the transient kingdoms on earth compared to Papal authority, which by divine decree rules over souls and bodies and has at its feet the whole world, Paradise and Hades? Who would dare to compare Semiramis, Morgana, Joan of Arc or any other heroine with our Joan? Nor do we have any ready point of comparison, for whenever a man surpasses his fellows in any quality, he may only be compared to an animal; to an ox, if a great king, to an ass, if courageous,[9] to a fox if a distinguished diplomat, but I know not to what animal if he becomes Pope.

The morning coolness and the braying of the donkeys bringing the next day's vegetables to her subjects interrupted Joan's ambitious musings, who, closing the window, returned to her bed. Rising the next day at around ten in keeping with the papal custom, she

---

[9] Well-known are the Homeric verses in which Agamemnon and Ajax are compared to an ox and an ass.

washed her hands and hastened to take up the reins of the state. She required but a few days to learn the art of popery. After less than a week of her having ascended to the apostolic throne, everyone was able to recognize clearly written on her brow "thou shalt have no other gods before me". No one prior to this Pontiff extended his feet to be kissed with more Christian humility; yet Joan, as a woman, was from long before accustomed to this. Truly remarkable was the dexterity with which she knew how to combine temporal and spiritual authority; in the name of Jesus taxing by means of the tax-collector and executing by means of the executioner, and in addition seizing and imprisoning and doing whatever else relates to the art of actively ruling. And do not think, dear reader, that I refer to these things in order to accuse her, but simply as the unpleasant exigencies of her position, to which Joan subjected herself with Christian patience. Women, those incarnate mixtures of love, devotion, mercy and all the other tender qualities, submerge themselves in blood as in a fragrant bath whenever the need arises. The Vestal Virgins, in other words the nuns of ancient Rome, would often invert their thumb to signify death to the vanquished gladiator; Saint Irene massacred thousands of men and blinded her own son; while the modest queens of England and Russia, Elizabeth and Catherine, made use of the axe and the knout with the same nonchalance with which they used their fans. Yet the popes, too, by divine right or rather by divine decree did the same. Hungry for some days, St. Peter fell into ecstasy and saw a screen, on which there were all the quadrupeds, reptiles and bipeds of creation and at the same time he heard a voice saying to him "Rise, Peter; kill, and eat."[10] This was the first revelation of the temporal power of the popes, who from that time killed and ate; and in order in every way to imitate the Apostle at whose feet the wealthy placed the proceeds from the sale of their lands,[11] the popes rendered all the world poor under the pretext of giving everything to the poor.[12] And if sometimes they murdered during the middle ages, they did so because in those times faith in the life hereafter rendered the present one of little value, nor did they feel any pangs of conscience when burning people, being certain that the Apostles too, if they had had executioners and wood, would have done the same.

According to the testimony of all the historians, Joan was, at least in the beginning, a good pope, observing all the traditions of her predecessors and tirelessly weaving that doctrinal net which was designed to conceal heaven from the eyes of the pious Christians. But no one at that time bothered to investigate whether that papal fabric was truly the heavenly vault. Bread and circus was what the ancient Romans demanded

---

[10] Acts 10, 13 and ff.

[11] Acts 4, 34.

[12] "They appropriated the greater part of the earth; on the pretext of giving everything to the poor, everyone was rendered poor." *Zosimus* Book 5, 13.

of their emperors, and their descendants demanded the same of their pope; but in Rome it was religion that took the place of the circus, while our heroine or rather His Holiness Pope John VIII, being young, an aesthete and ostentatious, took care to render the religious ceremonies ever more splendid. Night and day, the censers burned, the candles glowed, the bells rang and the people cheered. Only the Roman ladies complained occasionally about the Pontiff for not acting as they expected from one so young and comely, yet they hoped that he would quickly see and correct his mistake, following in this, too, the example of his predecessors and surrendering to them the keys of his heart and of his treasury.

Our heroine's intoxication with power and unparalleled activity lasted almost two years, during which time she ordained fourteen bishops, built five churches, added new articles of faith to the Creed,[13] wrote three books against the iconoclasts, cropped the Emperor Lothair, crowned his successor Louis and did many more things worthy of note, which with great admiration are recorded by the chroniclers, while those not wishing to accept Joan as pope attribute these to her predecessor or to her successor or simply erase them from papal history. This is how the Bourbonists dated the reign of Louis XVIII from the day of

---

[13] It was in this period that the Spanish addition of the *filioque* was rendered current in the churches of Rome.

his brother's death, ignoring as unworthy of note the laurels and imperial rule of Napoleon. Had the descendants of St. Louis prevailed to the end, had they succeeded in destroying all the statues of the Corsican and in erasing his name from all the books, as the Catholics attempted to do with Joan, who knows, "as time unfolds", whether that titan would have ended by being equally doubted and equally mythical as the titans before him, who piled mountains on mountains in order to besiege the heavens? After a thousand or two thousand years, when France like Greece has become a land of memories, perhaps some curious archaeologist will come to examine everything concerning Bonaparte, as today we are doing with Joan, and will inform his readers that in the dark ages of history there lived a courageous man who some called Napoleon and others Prometheus and who attempted to seize power from the kings and for this reason was chained to a lonely rock at the far ends of the earth, where an insatiable eagle by the name of Hudson[14] devoured his innards. But let us return to Joan.

Lofty social positions are like mountains, which from afar seem so harmonious in shape and bright in appearance, sometimes garbed in an immaculate veil of clouds and sometimes taking on a hue that reminds merchants of gold and kings of purple; but if one climbs to their peak, one is surrounded by nettles, thistles and

---

[14] Hudson Lowe, Napoleon's custodian on Saint Helena.

wild animals, and in Attica by brigands too. Such was the throne of St. Peter for our heroine. Besieged night and day by secretaries, toadies, courtiers and other suchlike greedy beggars, who circled thrones like crows do carcasses, she soon grew tired of extending her feet to those vile kisses and longingly thought of those golden days when, instead of her sandals, she extended her lips to the warm kisses of Frumentius. Ambition is like to a leech, which expires once it has drunk its fill. Joan had already begun to grow sick of the smell of incense as cooks do the aroma of roasted quails. She would often yawn while she celebrated mass in her gold finery before the altar of St. Peter and even while she was blessing Rome and the whole world[15] from the upper floors of the Vatican.

Yet while the vapours of ambition were dispersing, the old desires arose once again. Tedium softens women's hearts as heat does wax; while leisure and a full table have the same effect on the passions as oil does on fire. Aware of this, the ancient Egyptians sparingly meted out to their kings bread, meat, mattresses and hours of sleep, imposing on them, so that they would remain fit for ruling, much the same kind of diet that the English impose on their racehorses. Yet Peter's successors lived reclining on the down of swans and eating pyramids of partridges and hecatombs of venison, while on days of abstinence they ate flying

---

[15] *Urbi et orbi.*

fish, namely geese and duck, and in addition caviar, bulbs, oysters, truffles and other delicacies, supplementing those apples of Eden, which according to the rabbis contained beetles instead of pips. All this rendered our heroine a model of those constitutional monarchs, who like the gods of Epicurus snore on their lofty throne, surrendering the backs of the faithful flock to the shears of the ministers, just as, according to the Manicheans, the Creator surrendered the world to the jurisdiction of the Devil. Meanwhile, things (in Rome, I mean) were going from bad to worse; the wealth accumulated by Leo had been transformed into horses, litanies, banquets and sinecures, while the keepers of the papal treasury, though long having emptied it, did not hasten to distance themselves, but imitated Diogenes, who having drunk the wine shut himself inside the barrel. The Blessed John VIII, having become bored with state affairs and subjects and bulls and excommunications and other suchlike papal pastimes, had retired to Ostia, which was like Corfu for the popes of that time, and there, amidst a joyous group of beardless priests, he passed carefree days, lulled by the blue waves of the Mediterranean and the melodies of the flutes, lutes, three-stringed violins[16] and castrati, who followed His Holiness everywhere just as our deposed king is followed by the governmental portfolio and the welfare of his subjects.

---

[16] Violins at that time had only three strings.

Joan at that time was at the midpoint in her life, like Dante when he met the lion, the leopard and the wolf in the forest, but she, however, felt other beasts approaching no less fearful to women than wolves and lions, namely grey hairs and wrinkles. Her beauty was starting to sing, so to speak, its swansong. Yet, though eating so much forbidden fruit, she nevertheless still had all her teeth white and sound; while her appetites, sacrificed on the altar of her ambition, began once again to stir in her breasts, which no less than her teeth remained firm and well preserved. Often, summoning all her handsome courtiers to a luxurious banquet, she would pass before the rows of those cassocked Adonises after the meal, as the demure Catherine the Great did before the ranks of her bodyguards, halting before the one to whom she would offer the apple or rather to consider what would be the most discreet way of doing so. At other times, realizing the gravity of so bold an act, she would recoil in fear like a constitutional monarch before some arbitrary act, which is forbidden fruit for every constitutional Endymion. Joan gave little concern to the extent of the impiety and even less did she fear the verdict of the heavenly court, which punishes momentary weaknesses with eternal fire, boiling anyone causing sadness or pleasure to his fellow in the same cauldron. Being an experienced and clever woman, she could not believe that God had placed such bountiful things on earth simply for us to abstain from them, in the way that grapes are placed at English banquets for decoration and not to be eaten, yet she feared the scandal, the pregnancy and the wicked tongues, these three "bodyguards" of female continence. If, however, men were sterile like mules and silent like fish, I think the daughters of Eve would allow them neither to sigh nor even take a breath.

For two whole months, Joan struggled against the demon, scattering chasteberry leaves on her bed just as the Athenians did during the festivities of Demeter, drinking infusions of water-lily in keeping with the counsels of Pliny, eating lettuce tips like St. John the Faster, and neglecting none of the medieval potions for suppressing the youthful longings which were springing up in her forty-year-old breasts like flowers among ruins. Yet these longings were rather like quicklime, which burns all the more, the more it is slaked. After every victory over the flesh, instead of chanting victory odes, Joan wept like Brutus after sacrificing his son for the good of his country. "One more victory such as this and we are lost," cried Pyrrhus, counting the number of his fallen soldiers. And Joan said much the same as she plucked three grey hairs from her head after a sleepless night. Already certain of her impending defeat, she thought it pointless to prolong the struggle, having chosen her conqueror some time before. Only a few moments before he had died, Saint Leo had bequeathed to her his only-begotten son, or rather nephew (for the sons of the popes were known in Rome as nephews, even more so when the popes also happened to be saints), who was a twenty-year old lad, fair like a Laconian dog and equally faithful to

Joan, who had made him her private valet, an important and much-envied position at that time. This papal
offspring was called Floros and he always slept in the
adjacent room to the apostolic chamber, ready to run
at the sound of the papal bell. Our heroine, like the ancient Athenians, was accustomed to acting on her
every wish without delay; but now she found herself
for the first time at a loss, for in vain did she seek to
discover how she, as Pope, might extend anything
other than her sandals to the kisses of that young lad.
Often during the midnight hours, leaving her sleepless
bed and walking on tiptoe in her bare feet, she would
enter the room where Frumentius' designated successor was sleeping and, shading the light of the lamp
with her fingers, as the moon goddess did her beams
with clouds whenever she visited the Latmian shepherd, would remain for many hours gazing at the
sleeping youth. One evening she even dared to touch
his brow with her lips, before leaving in fear when she
saw his eyelids moving. The next day, the goodly
Floros recounted to his comrades how a nocturnal vision wrapped in an embroidered chemise had visited
him in his sleep. But visions, dreams and phantoms
were usual at that time just as today the souls of heroes
or even animals[17] reside in the mediums' tables, so that
rather than being surprised, most of them found lis-

---

[17] In the recent edition of his work (Paris 1863), the renowned
medium Allan Kardek teaches how it is possible to contact the
soul of his dead horse or dog. See *Livre des Mediums,* p. 376.

tening to the young valet's account actually tedious. Yet he, certain that his phantom was not of the usual kind, lay trembling in bed the next night and was unable to close his eyes. Everything had fallen silent in the papal residence apart from the owls and the clocks when a soft sound, like the flight of a night bird or the step of a young maiden hastening to her first tryst and afraid lest her virginal shoes should make any noise, came from outside the door to his room. The door opened silently as though pushed by a breath of air and the phantom approached his bed tiptoeing on bare feet. Floros felt his nightshirt wet with sweat that was cold like the waters of the Styx (I'm referring to the river in Arcadia and not the one in the netherworld, the waters of which are warm), the darkness only increased his fear, for this phantom was not self-illumined like other phantoms, nor was it carrying a lamp on that night, but rather it was barely discernible in the glow of the dying brazier like a pale and indistinct cloud that was slowly and menacingly approaching his bed. The cloud, the phantom, the ghoul, Joan that is, stood beside the bed and, encouraged by the stillness of the youth, began to lick the forbidden fruit with the tip of her tongue, not daring to bite into it. That touch instantly calmed the shudder running through the youth's veins and, coming round, he reached out both arms to grab hold of the phantom, which only just managed to escape, leaving part of its chemise in his hands together with five hairs of its head. But the goodly Floros was not satisfied with these spoils; overcome with emotion and curiosity, his blood was up and his legs pursued the nocturnal apparition, which fled in haste. They ran around the room several times before the phantom became caught in the folds of its torn chemise or shroud and fell on the carpet beneath the open window. Floros then extended his arm once again, but instead of encountering bones, worms, rotting flesh or any of all the other classic attributes of ghouls, his hand touched a warm and smooth skin, which appeared to be in use as a case for a living and beating heart. Whereupon he extended his other arm, but at that very moment, the full moon appeared from behind a cloud shining on the face and the naked breasts of His Holiness Pope John VIII!

At this point, dear reader, I could, if I so wanted, borrow some of the ribald language of Abbot Casti, of the Blessed Pulche, of the most reverend Rabelais or of any other modest cleric, in order with this to add a little manure to my narrative, which is in danger of becoming barren like the fig tree of the Gospels; but not being a theologian or a priest or even a deacon, I doubt whether I have the right to dirty my hands and your hearing. The poet of Don Juan found himself in the same predicament when, after a long pursuit, the hand of his hero finally came to rest on the bare breast of his third or fourth heroine, rather like the Ark on Mount Ararat. Not knowing how it might be possible to describe in a seemly way what happened next, Byron abandoned the poem and poetry and, becoming a misanthrope and philhellene in desperation, rushed to his death in the marshes of Missolonghi. Whereas, given that I am writing a true story, I am obliged, whether I like it or not, to confess that things so progressed between Joan and Floros after all the necessary explanations that the cheeks of the Holy Virgin, which they forgot to cover, grew red from the shameful acts, those of St. Peter grew pale with rage, the icon of the crucified Christ fell from the wall and shattered, and the guardian angel of Pope John VIII, who had not yet realized that the holder of the keys to Paradise was a woman, flew up into heaven, covering his face with his wings. Had it been daytime when this sacrilege took place, without doubt there would have been an eclipse of the sun, just as when Caesar was murdered, Augustus died and Jesus was crucified; but because it was in the depths of night, the only thing that the truthful chroniclers were able to describe for us was the moon, which was obscured by blood-red clouds. According to others, the miracle was postponed till the following morning when the inhabitants of the eternal city waited in vain for the morning star to appear; so that there was a triple night as when Zeus sowed Hercules; though I very much doubt whether Joan found that night too long, for according to Solomon: "Neither Hades, nor fire, nor the love of a woman can ever be quenched."[18]

---

[18] Proverbs 30, 16. The Vulgate, translating faithfully from the Hebrew and disliking paraphrase, expresses it more literally: "Tria insaturrabilis, infernus, terra et os vulvae".

On the day after that triple night, when Pope John appeared to his courtiers, His Holiness' face was radiant, his mouth and hands lavishly dished out favours, sinecures and blessings, and this papal joy was reflected in the faces of the courtiers, who gladly raised their heads like ears of corn watered after a long draught. That day the ruler of all Christendom allotted four bishoprics, ordained sixteen deacons as priests, added two saints to the Calendar, pardoned five criminals sentenced to be hanged and twenty heretics condemned to the stake, and was sad not to have had a hundred hands like Briareos in order to hand out more favours. After this, Joan went to church and later received the emissaries of Prince Ansigisel, who was seeking help against the Saracens. Yet while she did all these things mechanically, her eyes were everywhere seeking Floros and her spirit fluttered around her bed like a bee around a blossom and often during the course of the day she muttered like the Prophet David: "Oh that I had wings like a dove! for then would I fly away, and be at rest."[19]

For two whole months Joan continued to glide like a swan on the sweet waters of endless pleasures and adored by her young lover, even if she had already passed life's midway stage, after which we longingly begin to look back. But Floros was still at that happy age in which even thorns seem fragrant to us and all

---

[19] Psalms 55, 6.

women beautiful, in which we offer our hearts and lips for auction, fearlessly throwing ourselves into any arms that open to us like Daniel into the lion's den, asking for water to quench our thirst and indifferent, like the Arabs, as to whether it is clean or murky with sand. Yet, though forty years old, our heroine was in no way unattractive, still having teeth that were whiter than her hair and having replaced the down and fragrance of youth with that voluptuous rotundity and imperious plumpness that so captivates beardless youths, who like to entrust the reins of their heart to firm and experienced hands. Many critics (whether orthodox or heretical I could not say) prefer the *Odyssey* to the *Iliad*; there are also painters who prefer ruins to modern buildings and gourmets who like their fowl high. So, too, many followers of Solomon claim that it is only mature ladies who know how to skillfully flavour the forbidden fruit, scattering blossom on the path leading to it just as the Jesuits do on the path to Paradise. When grown old, Petrarch dreamt of that ideal woman who would combine this art with flourishing youth and in vain did he wander through fields and forests searching for this chimera, which he called "succulent fruit on a young sapling"[20] But Floros had not yet begun to dream of white blackbirds and, though his Joan was forty, he would not have exchanged her for two twenty-year old maidens.

---

[20] *Frutto viril su giovenil fiore.*

Meanwhile, summer had long passed and the Holy Father was in no rush to return to his seat. The last leaves of the year were piling around the boles of the trees, the sea was roaring rather than whispering, the wolves were coming down from the hills, but the two lovers remained joyful and playful, like lovebirds in spring. Many philosophers have endeavoured to discover what difference exists between man and beast. The Jews maintained that there is no difference,[21] the Christians that man has an immortal soul, the philosophers that he is a rational being and Aristotle that he sneezes more often than other animals.[22] But better than all, in my opinion, was Socrates, who observed that we surpass animals in one thing, namely that what animals do only in spring, man is able to do throughout the year.[23] In order to justify his extravagant conjugal demands, Zeus ordered the earth to put forth blossom whenever he desired to engage with Hera in "intercourse" (in the sense that is given to this noun by Mr Philip Ioannou), thereby attributing the blame to the influence of spring. Joan, however, unable to manage such a miracle, replaced the rays of the spring sun with logs and candles, the fragrance of the flowers with aloe and cinnamon and the warbling of the birds with flutes and canticles. The banquets,

---

[21] "...yea, they have all one breath; so that a man hath no preeminence above a beast: for all is vanity." Ecclesiastes 3, 19.

[22] Aristotle, *Problems* II, LI.

[23] Xenophon, *Memorabilia* XXX, IV.

dice, monkeys, mimics, jesters and all the other forms of medieval amusement ceaselessly followed one after the other in the papal palace, while, according to some chroniclers, Bacchanalian odes and the stomping of dancers were often to be heard inside there. The Pope was never present any more at matins, following Solomon's: "In vain do we awake in the early morning",[24] herself composing prayers, liturgies and services[25] in accordance with what is stated in the Gospels, forbidding Christians to talk drivel; while often, freeing herself from her beloved's embrace after a thrice-blessed night, it happened that she would modify the *Paternoster*, just as she had adulterated the Creed, and instead of saying "our daily bread", she would ask the Heavenly Father to give her "her daily Floros".

A certain king of Persia, whether Cyrus or Cambyses or Xerxes or Khosrow I do not recall, promised a handsome reward for whoever would find him a new form of pleasure. For myself I would gladly settle for all those existing since the fall of Adam, but the bad thing is that not even these are lasting. Either the sweet cup escapes our reach before we are able to quench our thirst or the divine nectar it contains is

---

[24] Psalms 108, 2.

[25] These Liturgies were preserved at least until the 16th century, when they were seen by Felix Amerlinos and Martin the Frank; copies most probably exist even today in the inner recesses of the Vatican Library.

transformed into vinegar and so we turn away our lips in disgust. Our heroine, while sailing with all sails set on a sea of pleasure, suddenly ran upon a terrible reef which she had long before ceased to fear. The ten years of cohabitation with Frumentius and his rivals had more or less convinced her that it was possible for her to eat as many forbidden apples as she wished without fear of her belly swelling. Not having opened the Scripture for a long time, she had forgotten that almost all the Biblical heroines, Sarah, Rebekah, Rachel and the others, were barren until old age before giving birth to patriarchs and prophets. Consequently, she was greatly perplexed when the symptoms described in the fourth book of Aristotle informed her, as the angel did Samson's mother,[26] that the Almighty had finally blessed her womb. But while the Jewess jumped with joy at the first stirring of her son, Joan, in her alarm, dropped the cup that she was bringing to her lips, and while her table companions viewed the spilt wine as a portend of good fortune, she ran to her chamber, shut herself inside and began to bewail her misfortune.

All eyes had long closed in the papal palace, but Joan was still awake with her head in her hands, like St. Peter after denying Christ, as in vain she sought a way to avoid the danger threatening her. Perhaps she

---

[26] "And the angel of the Lord appeared unto the woman, and said unto her, Behold now, thou art barren, and bearest not: but thou shalt conceive, and bear a son." Judges 13, 3.

might desert Rome and the keys to Paradise and, together with Floros, leave for some unknown corner of the world, or perhaps through incantations and potions she might expel the annoying and uninvited lodger from her belly. But both plans involved many difficulties and drawbacks, for she had no wish to lose the apostolic see, but nor was she willing to endanger her life and she was unable to find any other solution to this thorny problem. Her head felt heavy, her ears were buzzing and passing before her eyes were those flashes and shadows that the Stagirite philosopher regarded as irrefutable signs of pregnancy, when suddenly she heard a great flapping of wings. At the sound, Joan raised her head and saw standing before her a white-winged youth, garbed in a shining robe, with a halo around his head, a red candle in his right hand and a cup in his left. Never having seen an angel before other than in an icon, our heroine was so alarmed by the vision that she was unable even to rise to welcome the stranger or to even offer him a chair. Nevertheless, folding his wings and brushing aside the golden locks falling over his brow, the celestial envoy said to Joan as he cast a burning look at the wretched popess, "this candle represents eternal fire as punishment for your sins, the cup your untimely death and disgrace on earth. Choose between them." This angelic proposition caused great perplexity in our poor heroine, who for some time vacillated like David when he had to choose between hunger, war and plague. The fear of death and the terror of Hell struggled with each other in the breast of poor Joan just as Esau and Jacob did in the belly of Rebekah.[27] Initially she reached out towards the burning torch, ready to sacrifice her future life for the present one, but there was such wild howling from the infernal spirits, which are invisible but always present during such scenes, and the angel's countenance darkened so much that, changing her mind, she reached out and took hold of the cup of disgrace and drained it to the dregs.

This, my dear reader, is what the goodly chroniclers relate, whereas if you belong to the school of the Rationalists, who explain the miracles in the Scriptures by natural causes as Plato does the things of mythology, claiming that the star guiding the Magi was simply a lamp, that the angel bearing a lily for the Holy Virgin was a disguised lover,[28] and that Lazarus was only sleeping deeply when he was resurrected by Jesus, you might very well suppose, if, as I said, you belong to this

---

[27] See Genesis 25, 22.

[28] The Jews and their imitators, unable to accept the idea taken from Greek mythology of a god spawning children, fashioned a myth according to which the angel appearing to the Holy Virgin was in fact a soldier named Panther, who made use of this stratagem in order to engage her in "intercourse". See Talmud Legend III, by Eliphas Levi, *Livres des Esprits*, p. 61. This explanation was also accepted in Germany by the School of Rationalists, who accept the truth of the gospel miracles but explain them by natural causes. Strauss in the last edition of his work (Paris 1865, p. 61) is duly aggrieved by this interpretation of the Gospels, neither believing them nor thanking their critics.

school, that Joan saw the angel in her sleep or that some playful Deacon, having learned her secret, had equipped himself with two wings in order to frighten her. If, however, you prefer the system of Strauss, who, rather than waste time seeking explanations for inexplicable things, found it less toilsome to refer to as myths both miracles and the Gospels, you may see our heroine's vision as a simple invention on the part of her cassocked biographers. As for me, not belonging to any school, I prefer to believe what I have read, for as Solomon says: "the simple believeth every word".[29]

When, the next day, Floros came to the papal bedchamber, he found His Holiness lying on the carpet and suffering terrible convulsions. In vain did the poor youth try with his lips, like another Pygmalion, to warm his beloved, petrified as she was by fear. For two whole weeks Joan was confined to her bed, hovering between life and death. When, after that long struggle, she finally rose, she hastened to return to Rome and, shutting herself in her private chapel, she forbade entry to all her courtiers and even to the rays of the sun. There, besieged night and day by horrible phantoms like Saul after seeing the shade of Samuel, she ended up a shadow of her former self, jumping whenever she heard a door creaking and swooning if an owl or crow squawked on the Vatican roof at night. The sight of the celestial inhabitants never profited

---

[29] Proverbs 14, 15.

the wretched mortals who were deigned worthy of seeing gods, angels or saints face to face. Semele was turned into flame by the rays of Zeus, Blessed Nicon was left with only one eye after looking upon the radiant beauty of the Madonna,[30] St. Paul was blinded by the light of Jesus[31] and Zacharias was struck dumb following the visitation by the Angel,[32] while the Jews were so fearful of visions that every evening before going to bed, they would implore the Almighty to protect them from those horrible "things that walk in darkness".[33]

Yet while the Pontiff was in fear of these otherworldly inhabitants, there were more terrible things threatening his power; the virulence of the Romans against him had reached its peak. The Italians at that time were not like the Constitutional nations of today, which regard their kings as mere architectural ornamentations placed on the top of the political edifice like statues on the roofs of the temples. Little concerning themselves with synonymical studies, they had not yet arrived at distinguishing between "reigning" and "ruling", but demanded that their ruler should rule

---

[30] See *The Salvation of Sinners*.

[31] "And when I could not see for the glory of that light, being led by the hand of them that were with me, I came into Damascus." (Acts 22, 11).

[32] "And when he came out, he could not speak unto them... for he beckoned unto them, and remained speechless." (Luke 1, 22).

[33] Psalms 90, 6.

just as their cook should cook. Seeing the coffers empty, the churches silent, the monasteries transformed into inns, the Saracens plundering the coasts and the brigands encamped on the outskirts of the holy city, the good people of Rome at first asked with astonishment, then with impatience and finally with anger, what His Holiness was doing and why, when there were so many enemies to be fought, he had left his temporal and spiritual weapons in their sheaths. The pious complained that he no longer bestowed blessings on them and the beggars that he no longer gave them their pottage of lentils; the fanatics stated that for the past six months not one magician or heretic had been put to the stake; and the lame, possessed and paralytics asked why the Pope no longer worked any miracles. Yet the ones most enraged with the Holy Father were the clerics without a parish, the abbots without a monastery, the "chancellors" and "constables", for whom there was no longer any place in the court, the parasites ousted from the papal kitchen, and above all the procurers and barbers who could not understand why they had been excluded from the palace when both custom and tradition demanded of the pope that he shave and womanise. All these, after often and in vain offering their devotion, their servitude, their razors and their protégées, finally lost all hope and turned into terrible adversaries. Unable to find a spoon in order to sup from the bowl of papal generosity, they sought to upend it, like the Indians uproot trees, in order to eat the fruits.

Yet it would seem that nature itself in that particular year had subversive tendencies. The Tiber overflowed, sweeping away dams, boats, towers and bridges; the flowers forgot to blossom and the cherries to ripen though it was already mid-May; while the birds remained silently perched on their boughs and downcast like the pious cocks of Jerusalem during Holy Week. But what most alarmed the Romans were the swarms of locusts, so dense that for eight days they blotted out the rays of the sun, while the sound of their wings was "as the sound of chariots of many horses running to battle."[34] These devastating insects had six wings, eight legs, long hair like women and venomous tails like scorpions. I am ignorant as to whether this is a historical description or whether it was borrowed by the chroniclers from Revelation like the Evangelists borrowed from the Old Testament for the New, but these locusts were so voracious that after devouring the corn and the trees, they swept into the homes and churches, devouring even the consecrated bread and the altar candles. And after devouring these, they began eating each other, fighting in the air with such fury that their bodies fell thicker than autumn hail and during those days there was not one Roman who dared to go outside without an umbrella, parasol, sunhat or raincoat.[35] At this last plague, the

---

[34] See Revalation 9, 9.

[35] Umbrellas, in the shape they have now, though always used by the Chinese, were introduced into Europe much later; yet be-

rancour of the faithful finally overflowed, relentless and torrential, like the waters of their flooded rivers. Certain that all it required was a gesture from the pope to rid them of those winged beasts, they asked each other in desperation why Christ's representative kept his all-powerful hands in the pockets of his robe and his subjects at the mercy of the locusts. As for the above-mentioned honourable factions of those in opposition, they opened wide their nostrils and greedily smelled the coming storm, like Arab steeds do the desert oases, and when the time was right, arraying the Roman rabble in phalanxes and companies, they led that howling mob to beneath the windows of the Vatican.

At the sight of the wild crowd, the guards rushed to barricade themselves behind the gates, while the courtiers hugged the crosses and icons as the Theban maidens did the idols of the Acropolis when the seven champions brandished their shields before the walls. Only Floros, who had been long deprived of his beloved, roaming day and night outside the locked door of her chapel like Adam outside his lost Paradise, jumped with joy at finally having a good excuse to cross that forbidden threshold. Poor Joan was sitting in one of the pews, like an Egyptian monk with her anxious gaze fixed on her swollen belly, coming

---

fore this, there were similar implements used against the rain and the sun. See in du Cange, *Glossarium mediae et infimae latinitatis*, the entries for "baldaquinum" and "umbrellam".

from which, however, instead of the Holy Spirit, she fully expected to see her shame and her disgrace, and it was only after much pleading that she consented to appear to her subjects in order to calm the storm. When the wan and altered figure of the Pontiff appeared at the window, lit by a faint ray of sun passing through the cloud of locusts, many of the insurgents, overcome by involuntary respect, bowed to the ground, as the standards of the Roman soldiers did before Christ when he appeared before Pilate, and yet there were also many impious hands raised with stones and rotten lemons and many Pharisaical lips that spewed out curses and insults against the representative of Jesus. Extending his holy arm to quiet the crowd, the Pontiff announced that the next day, when the Rogations began, he would anathematize the locusts in an official ceremony and, at the same time, he would do the same with anyone not returning to their homes immediately. This papal promise immediately dissolved the worries and calmed the anger of the good people of Rome, whose uproar had come to resemble those storms of the Propontis, which, according to Aristotle, might be calmed with just a few drops of oil.

The next day, everyone was up and about in the palace from early morning. The prelates were preparing their gold vestments, the deacons were cleaning the bowls and the grooms the mules, while in the square a crowd of devout Romans were rubbing their hands in joy. The Rogations were, like most of the Christian ceremonies, a legacy from the pagans who, at that same time of year, performed sacrifices for the fertility of the fields, dancing and carousing around the altars to Demeter and Bacchus, whose blessing they sought for the corn, the vines and the turnips. As for their descendants, they, through similar rituals, sought the protection of Our Lady of Plenty and of St. Martin, thus replacing Demeter and Bacchus. Yet that day the ceremony would be a double one, with the addition to the Rogations of the anathema against the locusts. In that golden age of faith, not only wicked people, but all the wicked animals (rats, crows, boars, worms, grubs and fleas) were subject to the anathema of the Church whenever they dared to eat the lettuces or disturb the sleep of the faithful. The number and maliciousness of the locusts rendered the anathema against them an official and fearful rite, at which all the devout Christians in Rome and the environs rushed to be present.

While the courtiers jostled expectantly and noisily in the Vatican's cloisters and passageways, Joan tearfully bid farewell to her lover. Our poor heroine had spent a difficult and sleepless night in her chapel, sometimes contemplating the immortality of the soul, sometimes trying on her sacerdotal vestments in order to find which of these would be most suitable for hiding the scandalous size of her belly. The terrible words of the angel echoed frightfully in the ears of the wretched woman, who, having lost all her philosophical acumen following the angel's appearance, reflected in fear on the scales in which the Archangel Michael weighed souls, the Devil's blowpipe, the cauldrons, the charcoals, the whips and all the other instruments of the medieval Hell. Then she began thinking about the various philosophical systems, about reincarnation, the migration of souls to the moon and, finally, about earthquakes, locusts, leprosy and plague, coming each time to the same conclusion that God, though almighty, was wrong to create torment and grief in this world and demons and flames in the other. Such were the things our heroine contemplated during that night and more still, which I am obliged to omit in my haste to finish my tale. Were I a poet, I would say that my Pegasus had got wind of his stable and even against my will is whisking me towards it, but being a "prosaic" pedestrian, I am still justified in admitting that after so many wanderings I am tired and long for my stable, namely the denouement of my drama.

On seeing his beloved's pallor and anxiety, the goodly Floros sought in various ways to restrain her, tearfully imploring her to postpone the litany. But once she had accepted the bitter cup, Joan had to drain it to the last dregs. And, besides, it was impossible for her to do otherwise. The crowds camped beneath the palace were impatiently stamping their feet and the plumed mules their hooves; the candles were lit, the bells were pealing and the censers burning, while His Holiness the Pope, placing the triple crown on his head and taking hold of his pastoral staff, finally managed to wrestle free of his dearest's arms, filled with presentiments as black as the crows which flew above the head of Gracchus on the day of his death.

When the ruler of the faithful appeared in the Vatican forecourt, more than twenty thousand Romans were already lined up for the litany and, as soon as the Pope had mounted his mule, this endless human serpent began to slowly unwind its cassocked coils towards the church of St. John. At the head marched the standard-bearers carrying the crosses and icons of the patron saints of the city; after them came the bishops in purple, followed by the abbots and monks, who walked barefoot and bowing their ash-sprinkled heads to the ground; the nuns and deaconesses came next under the standard of St. Marcellinus, the married women under that of St. Euphemia and, finally, there came the half-naked and loose-haired maidens, but with downcast faces because the locusts had left neither roses nor narcissi, with which in those flourishing years of faith they were accustomed to adorning their heads and breasts for the official litanies. The lesser clergy, the soldiers and the populace came last, followed by a crowd of vendors and inn-keepers, who kindled the piety of the faithful with ale, mead and quince tea. The entire crowd was chanting hymns to Jesus and St. Peter, but because amongst the crowd there were newly-converted Saracens, German Benedictines, Greek monks, English theologians and many other foreigners, who had not had time to learn Latin and so chanted the hymns in their own language, it consisted of an odd cacophony, which the pious

Chateaubriand would undoubtedly have called "a most harmonious symphony of all nations to Christ."

Passing by Trajan's Column and skirting the amphitheatre of Flavius, it eventually came to a halt in the Lateran Square. On that day, according to the chroniclers, the heat and dust was such that the Devil himself would have bathed in holy water, while the bodies of the locusts, whose fight continued in the air, crackled horribly under the feet of the pilgrims and their beasts of burden. All this only increased the indisposition and anxiety of poor Joan, who could barely hold herself on her mule and who, apart from anything else, began to feel such turmoil in her belly that she twice stumbled as she was climbing the steps of the magnificent throne set up in the middle of the square so that from this elevation she would be able to hurl the anathema against the locusts. Her Holiness dipped the sprinkler in the holy water and sprayed north, south, east and west, then taking an ivory depiction of the Crucifixion, she raised it to make the sign of the cross in the atmosphere polluted by the locusts; but suddenly the holy cross fell from her hands and shattered on the ground and before long the Pontiff himself also fell, pale and half-dead, at the foot of the throne. At the sight of this, the faithful flock leapt in fear, clinging to each other like sheep gripped by the fear of wolves. Those holding the end of the papal gown rushed to help the ruler of the Church, who was groaning and writhing in the dust like a serpent cut in half. Some said that His Holiness had stepped on a mandrake root, others that a scorpion had stung him on his holy leg and others that he had eaten some poisonous mushrooms. Most of them, however, claimed that Her Holiness was possessed, while the Bishop of Porto, the grand exorcist in those times, rushed to sprinkle her with holy water commanding the wicked demon to choose another abode. The eyes of all the faithful were fixed on the Pontiff's pallid face, expecting to see the unclean spirit coming out of his mouth or his ear, but instead of the demon, a premature and stillborn baby suddenly slipped from between the legs of the ruler of Christendom! The priests supporting the Pope recoiled in horror, while the circle of onlookers tightened with people shrieking and crossing themselves. The women climbed onto the backs of the men and those riding animals lifted themselves up, while the deacons used their standards and crosses as clubs to open a path through the crowd. Some of the priests who were completely devoted to the Holy See sought to transform the crowd's frenzy into devoutness by shouting "it's a miracle!" in a loud voice and calling upon the faithful to show reverence. Yet such a miracle was unheard-of and unprecedented in the annals of Christian thaumaturgy, which had borrowed many wonders from paganism, but nonetheless did not consider it becoming to present any male saint as being with child and giving birth like the king of Olympus; so the voice of the devoted priests was drowned beneath the clamour of the frenzied mob, who were kicking, spitting and trying to throw both the popess and pope-spawn into the Tiber. Managing to push through the crowd, Floros held and supported poor Joan, who was becoming paler by the minute, till, raising her dying gaze to heaven, perhaps in order to remind the one abiding there that she had indeed drained the cup to its dregs, commended her spirit, whispering the words of Isaiah: "I gave my back to the smiters, and my cheeks to them that plucked off the hair: I hid not my face from shame and spitting."[36]

As soon as this sinful soul left its temporary abode, a horde of demons surged from the Abyss to seize their prey, which they considered had long been con-tracted to them, yet at the same time a legion of angels descended from heaven to repulse the wicked spirits, claiming that her repentance had erased any of Hell's rights. But the demons could not be persuaded and answered the angels' arguments with their horns, while the angels drew their swords. The battle between the spirits was at its peak, their weapons resounded like colliding clouds and it was raining blood on the faithful gathered in the square, when suddenly the angel who had appeared to Joan, cutting through the ranks of adversaries, took hold of her wretched soul, where exactly I cannot say, and riding on a cloud transported her... most probably to Purgatory. These miracles, dear reader, are related not by four fishermen, like those in Judaea, but by more than four hundred

---

[36] Isaiah 50, 6.

venerable and cassocked chroniclers. Before such a crowd of venerable witnesses, we bow our head, declaring together with St. Tertullian: "I believe these things because they are unbelievable."[37]

Poor Joan's body was buried together with her child at the spot where she had expired and a marble monument was erected there adorned with a statue of a woman giving birth. Floros became a hermit, while the pious pilgrims went thereafter by another route to the Lateran so as not to pollute their shoes by treading in the footsteps of the profane popess.

---

[37] *Credo, quia absurdum.*

MODERN
GREEK
CLASSICS

C. P. CAVAFY
Selected Poems
BILINGUAL EDITION
Translated by David Connolly

Cavafy is by far the most translated and well-known Greek poet internationally. Whether his subject matter is historical, philosophical or sensual, Cavafy's unique poetic voice is always recognizable by its ironical, suave, witty and world-weary tones.

ODYSSEUS ELYTIS
1979 NOBEL PRIZE FOR LITERATURE
In the Name of Luminosity and Transparency
With an Introduction by Dimitris Daskalopoulos

The poetry of Odysseus Elytis owes as much to the ancients and Byzantium as to the surrealists of the 1930s and the architecture of the Cyclades, bringing romantic modernism and structural experimentation to Greece. Collected here are the two speeches Elytis gave on his acceptance of the 1979 Nobel Prize for Literature.

NIKOS ENGONOPOULOS
Cafés and Comets After Midnight and Other Poems
BILINGUAL EDITION

Translated by David Connolly

Derided and maligned for his innovative and, at the time, often incomprehensible modernist experiments, Engonopoulos is today regarded as one of the most original artists of his generation and as a unique figure in Greek letters. In both his painting and poetry, he created a peculiarly Greek surrealism, a blending of the Dionysian and Apollonian.

ANDREAS LASKARATOS
Reflections
BILINGUAL EDITION

Translated by Simon Darragh
With an Introduction by Yorgos Y. Alisandratos

Andreas Laskaratos was a writer and poet, a social thinker and, in many ways, a controversialist. His *Reflections* sets out, in a series of calm, clear and pithy aphorisms, his uncompromising and finely reasoned beliefs on morality, justice, personal conduct, power, tradition, religion and government.

ALEXANDROS PAPADIAMANDIS
Fey Folk

Translated by David Connolly

Alexandros Papadiamandis holds a special place in the history of Modern Greek letters, but also in the heart of the ordinary reader. *Fey Folk* follows the humble lives of quaint, simple-hearted folk living in accordance with centuries-old traditions and customs, described here with both reverence and humour.

ALEXANDROS RANGAVIS
The Notary
Translated by Simon Darragh

A mystery set on the island of Cephalonia on the eve of the Greek Revolution of 1821, this classic work of Rangavis is an iconic tale of suspense and intrigue, love and murder. *The Notary* is Modern Greek literature's contribution to the tradition of early crime fiction, alongside E.T.A. Hoffman, Edgar Allan Poe and Wilkie Collins.

ANTONIS SAMARAKIS
The Flaw
Translated by Simon Darragh

A man is seized from his afternoon drink at the Cafe Sport by two agents of the Regime by car toward Special Branch Headquarters, and the interrogation that undoubtedly awaits him there. Part thriller and part political satire, *The Flaw* has been translated into more than thirty languages.

GEORGE SEFERIS
1963 NOBEL PRIZE FOR LITERATURE
Novel and Other Poems
BILINGUAL EDITION
Translated by Roderick Beaton

Often compared during his lifetime to T.S. Eliot, George Seferis is noted for his spare, laconic, dense and allusive verse in the Modernist idiom of the first half of the twentieth century. Seferis better than any other writer expresses the dilemma experienced by his countrymen then and now: how to be at once Greek and modern.

MAKIS TSITAS
God Is My Witness
Translated by Joshua Barley

A hilariously funny and achingly sad portrait of Greek society during the crisis years, as told by a lovable anti-hero. Fifty-year-old Chrysovalantis, who has recently lost his job and struggles with declining health, sets out to tell the story of his life, roaming the streets of Athens on Christmas Eve with nothing but a suitcase in hand.

ILIAS VENEZIS
Serenity
Translated by Joshua Barley

Inspired by the author's own experience of migration, the novel follows the journey of a group of Greek refugees from Asia Minor who settle in a village near Athens. It details the hatred of war, the love of nature that surrounds them, the hostility of their new neighbours and eventually their adaptation to a new life.

GEORGIOS VIZYENOS
Thracian Tales
Translated by Peter Mackridge

These short stories bring to life Vizyenos' native Thrace, a corner of Europe where Greece, Turkey and Bulgaria meet. Through masterful psychological portayals, each story keeps the reader in suspense to the very end: Where did Yorgis' grandfather travel on his only journey? What was Yorgis' mother's sin? Who was responsible for his brother's murder?

GEORGIOS VIZYENOS
Moskov Selim
Translated by Peter Mackridge

A novella by Georgios Vizyenos, one of Greece's best-loved writers, set in Thrace during the time of the Russo-Turkish War, whose outcome would decide the future of south-eastern Europe. *Moskov Selim* is a moving tale of kinship, despite the gulf of nationality and religion.

NIKIFOROS VRETTAKOS
Selected Poems   BILINGUAL EDITION
Translated by David Connolly

The poems of Vrettakos are firmly rooted in the Greek landscape and coloured by the Greek light, yet their themes and sentiment are ecumenical. His poetry offers a vision of the paradise that the world could be, but it is also imbued with a deep and painful awareness of the dark abyss that the world threatens to become.

AN ANTHOLOGY
Rebetika: Songs from   BILINGUAL EDITION
the Old Greek Underworld
Edited and translated by Katharine Butterworth
                    & Sara Schneider

The songs in this book are a sampling of the urban folk songs of Greece during the first half of the twentieth century. Often compared to American blues, rebetika songs are the creative expression of the *rebetes*, people living a marginal and often underworld existence on the fringes of established society.